Esthesis.

OTHER KOKOPELLIMA PRESS BOOKS BY ANGEL BRYNNER

Eutaxis   Ecclesia   Exodus

Erebus   Exist   Esthesis   Epicharis

Elision   Elysum   Empyrean

AOLAB active art decks & books BY ANGEL BRYNNER

ZION   HALCYON   DELUGE   BLOOD OF MY BLOOD

FLESH OF MY FLESH   BONE OF MY BONE

BLACKWATER   OVERFLOW   EDEN   ZENITH

AOLAB Travelogues BY ANGEL BRYNNER

BOTTOM OF THE NINTH WARD BULLETINS

BLACKWATER RISING

Anthologies BY ANGEL BRYNNER

FIRESTARTER   FIREWALKER

Grievechronic Revisionist AOLAB Active-Art books by Angel Brynner

DELUGE, ZION, HALCYON BLOOD FLESH& BONE ZENITH

Esthesis.

/grievechronic\

Angel Brynner

KOKOPELLIMA PRESS
MIAMI   NEW ORLEANS
KOKOPELLIMAPRESS.COM

Library of Congress
Cataloging-in-Publication Data
Brynner, Angel
Esthesis, grievechronic/ Angel Brynner
Library of Congress control number:2019956720

ISBN:

Audiobook edition
ISBN: 978-1-950077-55-7
Copyright © 2026 Angel Brynner

First edition
ISBN:978-1-950077-02-1
Copyright © 2007 Angel Brynner

Cover and book design by AOLAB. Additional artwork credit:
MACROVECTOR/FREEPIK, 4045/FREEPIK| FREEPIK AI

KOKOPELLIMA PRESS
MIAMI   NEW ORLEANS
KOKOPELLIMAPRESS.COM

Esthesis.

For all those lost in the fucked up shit they
were born into.

...and for the battle cries that erupt when
pain stops being enough.

" Don't worry, little girl...
their bad ways can't break your world. Tell
your story, you will see Things that roughly
Set you free.
Demons run and monsters scream, Life's like
Hell so reign in dreams. Don't you worry,
precious pearl... with your roar you'll rule
your world."
The feelings will bloom...
Or they will burn everything down. ...but you
Will begin again.
In the end.

Esthesis.

chapter one

"Why am I here?"

She spun around on her heels in a sloppy, self-taught pirouette and looked up at the One always alongside her. It shrugged its shoulders.

"Is this a Bad place?" she asked precociously. It shook its head no.

"Should I be afraid?" she pressed too pensively to be written off as the mere child she appeared to be. It shook its head no and boldly smiled through the ether, the way most things do when they can be heard but not seen.

"You should be." she whispered softly as she stared right where the eyes of the lurking spirit would be, taking it off guard. It's stomach began to growl as it hungrily leaned in towards the little girl. Irritated by its invasion of her space, she scowled and leaned back.

It laughed a little in surprise as curiosity got the best of it. A menacing growl echoed around them as it opened its mouth wide, showing all its teeth. "Why?" It asked.

"Because... I know what you are now." the little girl snarled as she whipped out a knife and slashed the demon to bits right before snapping out of the nightmare.

chapter two

Weary- eyed and defiant, lil Anukai sat up in her bed from the nightmare she'd somehow figured out how to turn back into just a dream.

She looked around in the half-light. The house was quiet except for the soft, circular snoring of her baby sister Flower in the crib she was technically too big for but that kept her safe. "Sunday," she yawned and tucked back under the covers.

Everyday except Sundays the father carted his last child to squat classrooms full of condescending behavioral education specialists by the time Anukai woke up. On Sundays she was always awake before he peeked in to check on them.

She heard him shuffling down the hall towards their door and quickly rammed pillows under her blanket. She looked around the room, tiptoed to the closet, thought the better of it, cracked it open and dove quietly under the crib.

The father poked his head in and cased the joint like Shaft before he sauntered over to where Anukai should've been sleeping and roughly dropped a Bionic elbow onto the bed, grimacing like the Junkyard Dog. Anukai slammed her hands over her mouth to stop from laughing out loud.

"Hmph! Pillows? You forgot you're a foot longer than this now, kid~" he grunted as he looked around the bedroom and saw the partially closed closet door. He grinned malevolently.

"Hey Durdee!" Flower sung out cagily from her crib.

"Morning, tree-be," the father sung out as he walked over. Flower scowled his scowl back up at him.

"Nuh." she grunted, having none of that. He knew her name.

"Not tree-be?" he asked innocently. She shook her head no and grabbed the bars to her prison. "Ah, you want out?" he murmured. His own grin erupted across her face up at him like the rising sun. "Well... you can't" he said seriously.

Flower looked at him darkly and shook the bars of her cell like a maniac. "Wait- wait~ You Can...but first...you gotta dime out your big sister."

"...Nuh." Flower whispered with no intention to help him. "Ah come on!" he fussed. "She's in the closet, ain't she?" he whispered and tiptoed towards it. Never taking an eye off her dad, Flower slipped her hand through the bars of the crib. Anukai flicked Flower's fingers as their dad charged into the walk-in closet wildly, slid out of her hiding place and set her kid sister free. She almost dove under her bed before scurrying back under the crib instead.

The father charged back out the closet and stopped short. Flower looked up at him and grinned again. "How did you even-" he started, then roared wildly, lifting Anukai's bed with one arm. Flower clapped happily.

He scooped her up and put her back in her crib. Soon as Flower started to shake the bars Anukai icy fingers darted around her dad's ankles and he jumped and fell on the floor, screaming like he'd been shot.

chapter three

For the millionth time little Gabryl fought his way up out of the morphine-induced haze they kept him in.

He stretched out his fingers and winced, which made him take in more air than his ripped lungs could manage without pain, but he refused to cry out. Because he was strong now, he told himself.

"Like a warrior. A Black one, too!" he muttered groggily. His eyes rolled back in his head as the face of the pedophile who had loomed over him in the alley flashed before him.

For the first time in what felt like forever, instead of cowering in fear Gabryl bared his teeth and violently lunged at the spirit of the man who had grown used to hanging out beside his hospital bed. Shocked, the demon finally fled from his side.

Gabryl's breath caught in his throat as he exhaled roughly. "It-it-it really Does Work!" he stammered.

The last thing he heard before he passed out into a fit of dreams was the voice of the suicidal woman with the tangled, black hair that shared the hospital recovery room with him.

"Told you~" she said hoarsely. "It's the only thing that does-"

chapter four

They treated his baby like a lab rat and him like the reason she was broken every time he dropped Flower off, even as the entire family continued the applied behavioral analysis therapy at home and she got better.

The weight of their silent accusations that his clair-sentience made him unable to ignore wore the last bit of resolve off of him, made him feel his quiet magic was useless against all this. The father's faltering of faith in his own abilities amplified his belief in the unspoken of magic of his firstborn. He did his best to bribe Anukai to do whatever it was she did that brought his lovely Flower out of the strange fog she had wandered into.

Only after he gave Anukai full access to every pastime and territory of his within the house did she play with Flower nonstop. She even let her little sister's horde of dolls be in her movies. Anukai's demands for things seemed grand from her child-like spot in the scheme of things but they were easy for him to satisfy. Each request the father made for help bringing Flower back home was met with a newfangled bargain, intense negotiating that stretched the child's comprehension, imagination and attention to detail. She haggled for it all, even down to absent-minded voyeurism during pot-headed chessboard crusades against D, his best friend and cousin, peaceably making movies with the captured pieces on the floor as full-fledged battles waged overhead.

She even learned how to play chess from absently hearing them argue over moves as she played with rooks, inhaling enough THC to stun a bull moose so often that she eventually became immune to it.

She'd giggle through playing her dad and flip into a militant, strategic hellion against D, who was always shocked at what she had picked up not paying attention.

It all bolstered Anukai's confidence in her own worth and abilities as she danced through the sometimes violent rooms of their family home, beaming with the pride of VIP entry to his very private world in a way that made the mother seethe.

Anukai worshipped her daddy because she knew in her heart that he at least he loved her and that she was only here because he'd asked for her. She was important to him, somebody real, who lived outside of her head. The joy that love birthed in her literally had her kissing his ashy feet in adoration at the end of long days, curled up around his eczema scarred legs like whatever the mother had done to break her that day had been useless. She sneered as she looked on.

"Look at her! Kissing your ugly, ashy, smelly feet like a dog! That's why I make her eat on the floor-" the mother snapped.

"At least someone is happy to see me when I get home," the father happily replied, calmed by the child. Convicted, the mother stormed out of the room as Anukai smiled up at him, sleepy, refusing to think about the hell there would be to pay once he left for work again.

"Don't forget- a Wolf-dog, Daddy, or I don't want it! It has to be a- a Timber wooolf-" she howled softly.

"I know, a wolf-dog-I'll try to find one." the father murmured groggily as Flower sat next to him on the couch.

Her tiny back was pressed so deeply into the cushions that her head hung at a strange angle that belied her wails of disturbed comfort whenever he tried to re-adjust her.

"No! Leave her be! She feels us here when she's smushed like that-" Anukai said with authority. "Now- Daddy, don't TRY-

There is no Try, Daddy, remember?! A wolf-dog! Timber wolf! Or Siberian Husky wolf! Pay attention- Daddy!"

The father taught her everything she ever could want to learn, and in ways that made her want to learn more just to blush-grin as she showed him what she'd done with it. She learned to cook next to him when the mother petulantly refused to make dinner. She started to love the hair on her head that the mother hated because out of nowhere he started to do it gently when they both sat bored out of their minds at his mother in law's Kingdom Hall of Jehovah Witnesses, and he taught her to do it herself by taking it down later so she could repeat it, his own wild Afro waving to the Earth Wind and Fire playing around them that kept Flower calm.

It was him who told her to draw what she saw no matter what. He demanded she pay attention to every vein in his beat up but pretty hands until she could capture what each finger, nail and pore looked like to her, regardless of how they might be seen by anyone else.

It all made the mother go from red with outrage to green with envy, obstinate even as her husbands' adoration of his first child eased the grip on the family of the stillborn state Flower had slipped into.

"The only opinion you pay any mind to beyond your own is Anukai's!"

"Because she thinks Right! & She actually gives a fuck about something other than what her flaky friends think-"

"Of course you think that! She just parrots your crazy ass! She's a stupid fucking kid!" Neither of them would be forgiven for calling the mother like they saw her, even when she saw it herself. Ever.

"Yeah- and even a stupid- assed kid can see how fake your flaky-assed friends are." he snorted.

But he didn't listen to any of Anukai's exasperated cries about why she thought Flower had gone away in the first place. In fact, it was the only place he ever tiptoed around. Every enraged accusation Anukai lobbed against his youngest sister Tsunga without the right words to explain it was outright ignored. So much so that it weirdly helped her to do the same.

Anukai started to treat it like it was all a weird glitch, a blip on the already tremulous surface of strained things, even though she could not forget what continued to happen to her under the leery hands of the Tsunga nor erase the suspicion that the Tsunga was now attacking Flower too.

Whenever Anukai's plodding, repetitive ABA play with Flower was interrupted by them piling into the car to head to their grandfather's house to be watched, she became whiny all the way there as her only means of protest.

Each time the kids were dropped off they pressed their faces against the dirty screen door that looked out onto the porch as their parents rolled away to try not to argue in public over things always just under the surface.

And every time, all inroads into keeping Flower out of her little black hole were blown to bits by the time they returned to take them home.

chapter five

Anukai kept her sister as close to her on the front porch as she could while their grandfather did his best to drink himself into the most opaque stupor possible right in front of them. The attempt to drown in gin worked against him, preserving his insides as if he were downing formaldehyde for his health.

He was a tall man, imposing like the tribe of minor gods and goddesses he had spawned. To Anukai, his skin was the color of oil smeared across the prettiest shade of car rust she had ever looked at, a supernatural sheen of life he was hell- bent on knocking off in shame. He stared balefully at the two of them on his turf from his demoralized and grief- stricken throne, emptying bottle after bottle.

Her eyes darted like a pendulum between his swigs from his gin bottles and the bizarre actions that spurted out of Flower as she grappled with following Anukai's repetitive ABA lead in the shade.

Under her flinty gaze the lines of her grandfather's face seemed to cut deeper. She thought he was beautiful, the most regal ole man she'd ever seen. He reminded Anukai of the chiefs carved out of oaks and chained to general stores in the boonies, wood roughly stained highly unlikely hues of red ochre and burnt sienna signaling protection, welcome, and willingness to wage war. Except with him the color was natively his, though he was likely to have only one Ouachita chief for every two Tuareg represented in bloodlines he never wanted to talk about. Especially not with his 'so curious it was obscene' first grandkid who shouldn't know how to see the "something else" in his skin in the first place as far as he was concerned.

If it wasn't for recalling against his will where his first boy (her dad) had inherited his own oversight from he'd have been more alarmed. The effects of the firewater on his system spoke volumes about his genealogy, regardless.

He tried to flare up to make his grandchildren go away, his thunderous voice erupting the way that used to send his own kids scrambling and still kept his youngest, the do nothing teenaged Tsunga lurking on the far edges of the property as far away from her drunk father as she could possibly be while still sending out an animalistic stench that Anukai warily picked up in the air. But his roar was the only voice that his grandkids knew him to have, so they just thought he talked that way. They sat there as if the howl was a melody sweet to their senses. He had so many children that the torrent of names that spilled out of him in rage rarely contained any indication that he actually was speaking to them anyway.

Eventually he gave up banishing them back into the house due to the panicked look in Anukai's eyes each time he barked that he was about to do it, irked by their play drowning out his pain that hounded him. It had been a life lived hard and he felt he had nothing left.

He'd gone from lying about his age for the opportunity to be a third-class citizen in the Army due to Good Ole Boys respecting the Japs for hitting their American Dream at Pearl Harbor more than they did the Black men fighting alongside them to having to fight those same Sons of Bitches tooth and nail for the rights to that American dream afterwards in their own land, even though it was Black men like him and the Asian Americans that Uncle Sam forced to prove they weren't the enemy that were the only reasons the USA even won in Italy.

After returning home in the post traumatic shambles of battle fatigue with the promise of being a hero for helping the world avert a global atomic catastrophe in the Pacific Theater turning out to be another white lie due to Jim Crow shit, he stoked a nuclear war at home, one he balefully kept going for decades.

Post-war, he'd lived through a smattering of years watching extended family members fleeing the ashes of black towns white neighboring hamlets had burned to the ground out of jealousy over them doing just fine without them. Childhood friends and cousins got lynched, shot or re-enslaved by fear, families ripped apart again by mandates to Go North or die. He'd fought obstinately against all that. He had inherited property. That he could do something with if given the space to breathe.

Then the wife of one of those Good Ole boys had slapped his burgundy black face for rejecting her attempt to Mandingo him. And he'd slapped her back, enraged at her dishonoring his butter yellow wife with her attempt. He and the woman he'd then ferociously loved had to run for their lives with their three small children under the cover of night.

He'd never dealt with the fact that loving her uprooted him from everything else that mattered or that standing up for her like the hero he was, that this country never let him be when he came back seemed to all but ruin his life. He blamed her and made her pay by philandering the way he'd refused to in the first place, trying to prove that love didn't rule him any longer.

It was to no avail.

She fought him back every step of the way, birthing a slew of giant children between battles. He had literally stolen her peace and killed her every joy with his words and cheating in the past, getting put out again and again.

But when the whoring and the verbal slaps he'd spent decades hurling at her escalated to him putting his hands on her, he mysteriously showed up and collapsed on an emergency room floor on the other side of Cleveland, mute, covered in blood, a bullet lodged in his head. He'd awakened paralyzed and unable to speak as his scrambled brain re-wired itself and the doctors tried to figure out how to gingerly extract the bullet.

Like the dutiful, long-suffering wife married to a hellion that everyone knew her to be, she'd solemnly nursed him back to health in the hospital in front of everybody, almost dotingly. To stay abreast of any developments in the case.

With no leads, the cops never found the gun or the assailant. "Maybe now he'll see the good woman he has in her~" the nurses had loudly whispered to each other as they'd watched her lean in and kiss him on his stiff forehead, eyes glowing.

"...Of course he does-Look at the fiery love shooting from his eyes! Think of all twelve of those kids- they must be so happy-"

He was still haunted by the elegant, Erte-esque swoop of her neck he'd completely forgotten about in all his antics and abuse as she'd followed his glance towards the nurses and nodded, sending them away. Her eyes had danced across their children present, also excusing them one at a time as her gaze made its way back to him.

His wife's eyes had gleamed with more than the darkness he had sown within her for decades. She'd built upon it. He remembered every word she'd uttered.

"Shh~Don't..." she'd murmured, eyes on fire as she'd slid one of the many pillows propping him up just enough askew for it to press against the side of his nose and face closest to the door. "Don't try to speak now...it's too soon...and clearly you still have too much to say~" she'd smiled.

"You'll talk again."she'd whispered, hugging him and roughly pressing his mouth and nose into the pillow to slightly suffocate him. "You'll talk...when you recognize you better not say a thing, you hear me?"

He could still smell and taste the panicked sweat he'd broken into understanding that she'd kill him right there in the hospital and no one would be the wiser. That was one of the tastes he'd spent the remainder of his life pouring gin down his throat to erase.

"You Have to get better," she'd growled sweetly as she caressed his cheek. "...Because you have to go back to work. To feed all these fucking children you kept knocking me up with, even after the doctors told you I couldn't carry anymore," she'd whispered.

He'd laid there speechless, stricken and furious.

She'd pointedly missed killing him. On purpose. And they both knew it. Because she was the dead-shot of the two.

...He'd gotten better.

Which just made the war worse.

He raged, wounded by the monster he had to take full responsibility for creating, unable to say shit because it'd been his gun he'd illegally had that she'd shot him with and hid. When the cheating roared back out, she threw him out again.

"You'll be dead in six months if you let me come home again, like you always do, you worthless piece of ass-" he'd sneered.

Fed up, she ripped the soon-to-be from him with a little Logos magic of her own, sparks shooting from her eyes just like his. She finally cursed him back, in front of the entire prepubescent and teenaged brood, done.

"You think I'm worthless? Maybe you're right! Try raising these twelve of the 18 you made me carry On your own - the TWELVE that didn't die, that survived all This- and YOU- against all odds - You're nothing but a vicious drunk, with or without me!"she'd roared. "And they will be nothing without me, just like you- you angry sonafabitch- "

He'd laughed as he'd sauntered down the steps, waving off her standing in agreement with his curse at the time.

But six months to the day of sheepishly being allowed to come back home, his beloved's weary spirit gave out in her sleep, left thumb tucked into the corner of her fatigued mouth for the last time.

He had hovered above her cold, lifeless body that morning in shock as the demons he'd lorded over her with turned on him and carved the last combative thing she had ever said to him into every cell of his spirit. Seeing the light of his beloved go out the way he'd said it would that was the mortal blow to his soul.

He had always known that he had the Logos old folk used to know better than to talk about. But now he was one of them old folks and his unchecked supernatural ability had led to having to bury his long-suffering, actually once adored, forgotten fireball of a wife. Who had left him on this plane with a guilty, metallic taste in his mouth, twelve kids to care for, hordes of grandkids popping out all over the place... and the tiniest shard of a slug left in his brain.

That had been almost a decade ago, but he lived with the manifestation of both his and her vicious words pressing into him every day. He'd failed miserably as a single father and it was scrawled across his now grown children, strangers he looked out at from the shell of himself whenever they warily came near with their kids. All six of his daughters had found the same kind of berating man they'd known him to be to lay down with, reeling in the dust alongside their dead mother. The six sons had barely fared any better. He drank to not see what went on in his own house in the aftermath as his demons ran rip-shod over it.

"*Yes, you Are a God,*" his inner demons sneered whenever sobriety started to creep up. "Who *used his Logos to murder his godly wife. Even Zeus knew not to kill Hera!*"

Anukai had been the only grandchild she'd lived long enough to see.

And it was as if the grandmother's perfect aim and predilection for her left thumb well into old age transmigrated to Anukai with her passing, in a way that creeped everyone out.

chapter six

The old mad man mopped his brow with the t-shirt he had shoved in the pocket of dungarees so caked with love and life lived that they could have stood up on their own at the end of days.

"The streets of Heaven may be paved with gold but I'm telling ya...in paradise the roads are cut from rock that gleams like diamonds in the moonlight -" the man happily gabbed as they heaved boulders, in love with the exertion of service.

The little boy next to him huffed wordlessly. He struggled to lift another hunk of limestone that had to be cleared before the garden that was to be his could be planted.

"And in paradise, boy- the air is smoky and clear at the same time, like all the stuff you can't stand about yo'self being burnt off just by breathing in and out- Now, listen to me, boy-"

The little kid scrunched up the caterpillars he had for brows into a scowl. He tried so hard not to think bad words because he knew that he would be heard outside of his head and they ain't call the old man Mad for nothing. But even though his body wasn't tired, his young mind knew he should be, that tired or not, this would be called work with a capital W anyplace else but here.

They'd been pulling rocks out of moist, black dirt that never felt right on his skin. As the old man rambled on the boy's eyes fell to his dirty hands.

It felt heavy, laying there innocently enough until he narrowed his eyes in accusation at it, not trusting it at all.

As if sensing that the jig was up, the granules of black dirt in his palm double-helixed up softly then kicked up a tiny tornado that danced across the lines of one hand as he absently tried to keep working with his other.

"With a beauty that cuts through anything false in you like glass-" Old man Mad thundered.

"Son of a-!" the little boy cursed as he rammed his finger against the big boulder he felt like he'd been trying to move for forever. Then he froze, remembering where he was.

"Let me see it, son," the old man growled, brows knit in consternation that matched the look on the boy's face. Warily, the kid shook his head no.

"Give me your hand!" the old man boomed as his brows wagged more aggressively, love doing its best to flood out of his eyes and drown out the fear in the boy. Hesitantly, the boy extended his hand towards Old man Mad.

His finger was mangled, completely out of joint. Shock and fear rumbled through him, any pain a moot point until he was asked one question. "Does this hurt?"

He slammed his eyes shut, winced and vigorously shook his head yes as tears rose up by default and he began to bawl.

"Good, because I ain't even touched it yet." the old man said dryly. Shyly, the kid opened his eyes.

He stared at his now obscenely crooked finger and felt his stomach flip-flop.

"Good. Now pay attention. Yeah, now as I was saying,... in heaven, it's been said, ya know, that there's all these precious gems all over, but what you gone do with rubies, sapphires and such? Seems to me that kind of extravagance is gonna draw the wrong Kind o' folk as it is, least when I look at it scientifically.

Sure, they're precious and all but can you eat them stones? Can you, son?"

"..No?" the boy said, "I feel woozy-"
"Good, then its' workin, now pay attention- And would you- would you want a gate made out of pearls, or would you want some of those oysters they be shuckin' down the way that you love that they find pearls in?"

Old man Mad looked intently at the boy as he perked up, his hurt hand totally forgotten the instant oysters were mentioned.

"Oysters? Are we gonna have oysters because of my hand?! Because I Love oysters!-ooh~you know how I love oysters!" the little boy murmured as his mind wandered towards his empty belly.

"So it is safe to assume you are sayin you'd prefer oysters to a gate made out of some big-old pearl." Old man Mad mumbled.

"What's wrong with you, Mad? Why you keep talking 'bout pearls and sapphires and gold? And oysters?! And what's wrong with my hand?" the kid asked, confused.

"Nothin's wrong with your hand." The old man muttered.

"Of course there's something wrong with my- you saw it yourself-what do you mean? It's-" the boy fussed as he lifted his hand to show the old man that he was crazy.

"Look at it-" Mad muttered as he didn't even bother to look himself. The boy gasped as he stretched out his hand and his finger went right back in line with the others.

"But- but how did-how did you-" he stuttered.
"Told you to pay attention," Old man Mad grinned slyly. "You tricked me!" the boy argued as he waved his perfectly fine finger in Mad's face.

Mad clucked his tongue. "People say pay attention for a reason, sometimes even to make sure you'ont pay attention." Mad grinned and took the boy's hand again. "Want it back the other way?" he asked. Before the boy could answer, his finger disjointed again.

"Aww come on! Put it back right!" he fussed. "You do it." Mad grinned mildly.
"Me?! Ion't know how!"
"YOU did it last time!" Mad chuckled. "What? How? Me?! I did not!"

"Oysters~" Mad murmured.
"Oysters?! Ooh~ I love Oysters, stop making me think of- that -you're making me so hungry~ I remember last time we had oysters and-"

Mad slowly pointed to the boy's finger going back into place all on its own.
"But How~?" the kid whispered.

"Love-" Mad said simply. "Notha thing this place got on some so-called, posed to be heaven ANY day... Everything is made whole here. We are free to be whole here or not. Alla- time. Long as we love. Something. Understand?" Mad asked him.

The boy nodded solemnly. They got back to work in silence but it was obvious he was still a bit confused. Finally he just asked. "But Mad...If it's so great here, why we gotta move rocks anyway? It's like...work, isn't it?" he asked.

"Work's not bad, son. It's good for you...but this? It's not really work, anyway. It's like..." Old man Mad mused aloud, "Like Preparation... for more...better. Much-much mo'better. But we gotta face the bad that was so we can see it no longer is in first place-" Mad dusted his hands off on his thighs. "Come on then, let's go get you some of those oysters ova yonder that you act likes a part o'you."

"But why, Mad? Why we-"

"Because stones in good ground block the best growth, so they gotta come out, you see? Stones gotta be rolled away from tombs and gardens... for the light...the life to break back forth from the earth, you see? And you gotta learn how to build a garden, son. We all do, sooner or later. Or we gone end up feeding one-" Mad said softly as they headed down the road.

The little boy yawned and nodded as they went back over the hill to the place they'd come from, for the love of oysters over pearls.

chapter seven

The demand on Anukai to work for the solace his stupor offered them both was usually unspoken.

Corner store.
Kool cigarettes, an errand only agreed to when the man she affectionately called "Graindaddy" promised to keep Flower with him the entire time she was gone, no matter who did and or said what... with the threat to pour all his hooch down the sewer if he didn't keep his word.

"Come on Lexy-Tsunga- Cherie- Jessie- child! You know I'm talking to you! I need my cigarettes! I'll watch her- I won't let her out my sight- come on, now!" He rattled harshly. A nicotine fit threatened to break the haze of gin coating his spirit and the emphysema clogging his lungs due to a lapse in the tar coming into them. Anukai locked onto Graindaddy like his blood was as much hers as it was his no matter how much he thinned it out. Her stare burnt through the fumes in his head caused by a passively allergic reaction to the botanicals and juniper berries that coursed beneath his skin. Her wide-set, wet eyes cut him like his mother's had as a child when she'd caught him in a lie, sobering him up in a completely different way.

She gruffly yanked his left hand into both of hers and peered down into the palm of it, looking defiantly into the lines that shifted under her sight the same way they did under his own and then back up at him so he could see that she too could see whether or not he was in the midst of a lie. She inadvertently picked up on the tape he was berating himself with inside his head and her mouth dropped open in shock.

"Do you really think you killed her, Graindaddy?" Anukai whispered to him inside his own skull. The stoic man jumped.

He peered really hard at his first grandchild. His eyes looked really old to her for the very first time, like a piece of glass a bullet had just gone through without shattering yet.

"But I didn't mean to- I just hope she-" he found himself answering his granddaughter and himself inside his head at the same time.

"She knows." Anukai cried out softly. "You just gotta believe me she does... so you can be okay too. She's happy where she is...and she's sorry for what she said and did to you, too." Anukai sat stock-still, listening. "But she's laughing, she says you know you made her do it-"

Naked, but unashamed for the first time in ages since the tragedy had stuck, Graindaddy nodded, blushed and roughly struggled to pull Flower up into his lap as the toddler flapped her arms a bit slower than usual. Anukai went for his wallet then bounded down the stairs onto the block, looking more cautiously over her shoulder at the two of them than she did at the cars that zoomed by as she jay- walked across the street.

In Anukai's absence Flower chewed on the arms of her favorite toy as if the smell of her big sister in the stuffing sedated her. When she came back, Flower was peaceably asleep in her grandfather's lap as he looked at her, awestruck, flooded by all the memories that had been lost in the fires of life regarding how much of a comfort he'd once been to every child he'd held. He'd asked every one of all those mostly grown kids of his he complained about to come be his.

Anukai trusted Graindaddy from then on out.

Eventually he morphed into the baby-sitter he had never the time, space or gumption to be to his own kids. Even flat- out drunk he began to adore the company of little Anukai and Flower to no end. The Tsunga looked on jealously at what she'd never had with him, still avoiding Graindaddy at all costs.

Weeks passed. Soon even Anukai began to relax, thanks in part to the occasional sips of Gin that he gave her to slow the rapid fire intensity of her questions. Flower even stopped flapping her arms as they sat on the porch and basked in the setting sun, things back to the fragile normality that only families best at dysfunction can ever know.

chapter eight

The little boy rubbed his eyes. "Where is she? Where did she -"

He held his breath through the stench that rose off of everyone in Never-Neverland around him. He angrily pushed his way through the piles of dozing adults in the dark. The rooms and clumps of bodies seemed to go on forever as he made his way through the shot-gun style apartment in search of his mom.

"Mommy?" he whispered harshly as he pushed hair out of this and that face in search of her in the madness his young brain had already learned to steel itself against the way kids born in warzones instinctively learn to do.

When he could take any more, he squatted down like the little, lost boy that he was and quietly started to sob.

"Gahbloom-?" a woman cried out softly in response to her firstborn child's wails. "Baby-baby where are you?"she slurred, her tongue still thick with whatever she'd taken.

He looked up hesitantly, face wet with tears as he tried to decipher whether it was a dream or she was really there, unable to figure out where her voice was coming from. "Mommy?"

"Here-here I am, Gahbloomy~" she whispered from deep within a pile of bodies he had wandered past. "...here I am, baby-"

He ran to the pile and started screaming as he tried to claw his way in to her."Mommy!!Ma!Get off her!Get- OFF!" he howled.

"Yo! Somebody shut that motherfucking kid up!" a

disembodied voice bellowed as angry murmurs of agreement went up around them.

"Baby-baby-here I am-here I-come here-come here,baby-" the mother whispered weakly as she held up arms corroded with thin, dried rivulets of blood. The little boy crashed into his mother's arms and shook as he sobbed against her.

"Shhh~ Shhh,baby...it's alright...I'm here...I'm...I'm on my way back riight now-" she slurred.

chapter nine

"Hurry up!" The mother snapped. "I...I can't be late for this Toastmistress meeting. It's my turn to talk-"

Anukai pushed Flower into the backseat and tried to belt her in.

"Flower, stop fussing- we're going to see Graindaddy~ I can't wait- can you wait?"

Flower snort-laughed and shook her head no as she swatted at Anukai's hands,wanting to try to buckle the strap herself.

"Wait til he sees! " Anukai crowed. "He's going to be proud of you tying your shoes again, too!"

She was happy. She had started to miss him. They tumbled out of the car into the driveway and called for him.

But Graindaddy was gone. Anukai and Flower froze and looked up at the now grown Tsunga, the one that the parents had been paying to watch them all along, as she barreled menacingly out onto the porch.

Bewildered, both kids spun back towards their mother and started to throw temper tantrums.

"Shut it, Anukai." The mother hissed and drove off.

chapter ten

She came to as clumps of hair roughly tried to ram themselves further into the territory of her body.

Every orifice was clogged with it. If it wasn't for the ghastly sensation of every pore of her body gasping for air she would have surely suffocated as the rudimentary sensation of the torture shoved her towards insanity.

"***Recant!***" the Greek chorus roared around her in the dark.

She struggled against the irony of comprehending the request as they tortured her in a way that did not allow it, even if she would have taken back the accusation.

"**Recant!**" they screamed again.

The dismal echoing of the syllables slashed at the cord she barely held onto. She felt more hairs lash across her body, lacerating her skin as it snaked to bind her even tighter to the torture table. She screamed out hoarsely.

A soft cry other than her own split the atmosphere of the space and made everything stop hesitantly. She tried to lift her head from the slab but was roughly slammed back down.

Incensed at the interruption, her torturers redoubled their efforts, screaming at her to take back her testimony.

The soft cry broke through the cacophany again and she violently cried out towards the closest to salvation she'd ever heard.

"No! I'm- here!I'm-Get off me! Mama's- Noo!" she screamed. "Gabryl!" Gabr-"

The Inquisition leader furiously bashed her face in, making her tongue get cut by her already chipped teeth. Blood poured from her mouth as she roared, her r's becoming l's as she cried out for the one she now sensed on the other side of her madness, needing her.

chapter eleven

When the children were herded towards the car at the end of the night, Flower was a combustive mess of howls, rants and whines indicating an animalistic desire to go home.

Exhausted, the father went to pick up Flower and she snarled, gnashing her teeth at him. He jumped back, wounded, then wearily called out to a listless Anukai. "Get her, Anukai."

She angrily glared at her aunt and father then defiantly bolted out the house. She lunged into the backseat and slammed the door, covering her ears so as not to hear Flower's screeches or her mother's vitriolic snarls from the front seat.

The mother watched Anukai in the rearview mirror. "You Hear me talking to you!" the mother snapped. Anukai looked down in her lap then up at her mother in the mirror balefully. She'd had enough.

"*You told me to shut it,remember?...*" Anukai hissed telepathically as she locked eyes with the demonic woman who'd birthed her into this hell. "*...And You're going to pay for this- ALL of it.*" the child snarled as her eyes whited out in the mirror. The mother gasped.

They were jarred out of their strange communion by the father ripping open the car door. He pushed the front seat forward and did his best to gingerly secure Flower as she lunged at him like a rabid cat.

"Nuk- please help - come on-" he pleaded as Flower bit at him again.

Anukai rolled her eyes and clicked her tongue at her sister. "I'm sorry, Flower-" she cooed again and again, her eyes as weary as her dad's.

Flower calmed down as Anukai's lips made contact with the back of her head. "I'm Sorry, Flower-" she said again.

"Ah-sur-fluh" Flower muttered, wiped out.

They rode most of the way home in silence. Disgruntled by both the Tsunga's attacks and the continual collapse of all the hard work she did with Flower, by the time they turned onto their block Anukai broke, screeching in the back seat.

"Daddy-Why do you even keep having me fix Flower if you're gonna keep letting it happen again?! You keep taking us there! Are you stupid?!" she hissed, " Do you hate us too?!" Anukai cried, refusing to even look at the mother she knew with every bone of her body was letting it happen on purpose, at least to her.

Indignant, the mother cleared her throat to start to fuss when Anukai stopped her with one roar,ringing a bell that could never be un-rung. Her voice went metallic with rage.

"What's it gonna take for you to get it?! Who has to die before you get it? Nobody else was there! Are you stupid? I even told you- but you never listen! You never want to- So who has to die?! Which one of you has to die first ?! Because it won't be me! Or her! I'll kill everyone of you before I--" Anukai heaved, hyperventilating.

"What's it gonna take for you to stop it, Daddy?! Do I have to kill her to make her stop since You Won't?! Because I will! You'll all die! I know just how to, too-" Anukai screeched as her nails dug into the white vinyl back seat of the Monte Carlo.

Flower defiantly cried out next to her, her raw, incoherent voice even louder than Anukai's but obviously in key, her arms flailing wildly against the back of the seat as her big sister sobbed. "Ah-sur-fluh-!" she roared ferociously.

The father looked back at his children then squinted in disbelief as two and two were put together. The color drained from his face. He looked over at his wife.

She stared out the window, eyes bugged out of her head, indignant and incensed at Anukai's threat, but otherwise narcissistically ambivalent as their daughters melted down in the backseat.

He slowly pulled into the driveway, his grip on the wheel so tight that the imprint would never come out. The entire family sat in the car in the drive as it got dark, until the two little girls had worn themselves out. The mother was the first to open a door. She went to roughly reach over Anukai to grab Flower and both girls bared their teeth at her. She jumped back in angry shock.

"Screw this," the mother muttered and left him in the car with the kids. Not one thing was said about the day again.

chapter twelve

The crying child couldn't stop shivering in his mother's emaciated arms.

"You know-you know you're the blessed and best of me ...you know that right, little boy?" the mother whispered softly as she came to a bit more with each terrified shake of her son against her broken heart. "That's why I- that's why I call you my ...my Gahbloom~ because-"

She stopped.
Her senses came all the way back on with a slash of shame as where she'd come to with her poor child in her arms registered.

"Because- because I'm dirt-" she whispered harshly against the top of the little boy's head as the smell of the drug den raped her senses. "I'm- I'm nothing but-but fucking dirt- but...but you? You, baby? You are my flower- you're like a flower to me- you hear-you hear me? You're my proof God still loves me because he grew the goodness of you in the ground of me-" she whispered.

Her words sunk into them both. Then and there she decided to do her best by him by the grace of a God who had brought her viciously back to her senses via the sound of her child's sobs screeching outside of the hole she had crawled into. The demonic reality of the hell she had him in ripped across her. Everything around her demanded she fall back from her decision, but she refused. She might never forgive herself for the filth she'd come to in, but she was going to do right by him, give him the chance to be somebody. Even mothered by a broken soul like hers.

"You- you're gonna remember that, right?" she whispered

harshly. The boy sniffed loudly as his tears stopped. He nodded softly, feeling warmth push back into his mom's bony arms from the pit of a soul she had forgotten she'd had.

When the demons saw her tipping point had been crossed, they malevolently stirred up the carrion and cattle drugged out around the two of them. "Shut that fucking babbling up!" someone screamed.

"Yeah! And-Get that crying kid out of here!!" another woman wailed.

"Can we- can we go?" the little boy whispered. His mother nodded as she struggled to stand up in the abyss she had retreated into for the final time. Still hunched over, at the last moment she gently grabbed his face and kissed the streaks of the little boy's tears away. His face glowed with love for her as power flooded into his mother from the wetness of his tears on her lips. She straightened up all the way.

All of a sudden a gnarled old man in a nearby pile saw the little boy's glowing face and lost it at the sight of an angelic little cherub in the midst of his purchased Hell. "That light! That light!" the half-devoured man screeched.

"Get him out of here Now!Now!" another howled and lunged at them as little Gabryl's mother hugged him tighter in her arms. Strength blossomed out of nowhere and the mother swung on the man violently, knocking him to the ground with an explosive left hook.

"Get out! Get out before We all tear you apart!!" the gnarled man roared from the floor as the mother ran out of the drug den with her terrified child swinging wildly in her arms until she couldn't run anymore.

The streets of the city felt alien to her due to her all but permanent residency in never-neverland until now. She'd disconnected from it for so long that her panicked heart relied on nothing but built-in homing mechanisms as she sprinted like the wolves of her addiction were on her heels. She wasn't running from her disease for herself-she'd given up on herself the day she saw that no one who was supposed to cared enough to keep the beasts in the world at bay. She'd been as small as the all but catatonic child in her arms. She ran like a spirit stolen from the depths of hell on nothing but God-given hope for him.

When she looked up she was at the bottom of the stoop she used to play jacks on. Confused, she looked down at her son, her brain so garbled that she could not tell whether he was sleeping or passed out. She flew into a fit as sirens wailed in the streets around her. She frantically leaned on every bell until someone let her through the double doors. She slammed up the six flights of stairs, looking down hallway after hallway for something to jar her subconscious until she hit one that was familiar yet whited out of her memory at the same time. She froze in front of the door of her beleagured parents. The green paint on it glistened peacefully in contrast to the deep ecru walls and ebony trim of the hallway. Twisted visions of flames circled the red door down the hall where so much had gone wrong so long ago. They stabbed at the edge of her adult eyes as she banged at her parents' locked door then collapsed against it with her child knocked out in her arms. Gabryl was baptized by his mothers tears over nobody being home when she'd needed them to be once again.

chapter thirteen

As soon as their aunt was no longer allowed to baby-sit them Flower's tongue re-discovered the thousands of words she had known precociously ahead of schedule as it was. No one spoke on what had triggered Flower's swath of silence in the family, and the siblings began to traipse down the street alongside the other latch-key kids on the block, their older half-brother Seal leading the charge.

The parents made it up to the kids with pay-offs of a sort. Every special class a kid could hope to take on weekends now that they could afford it, dining out at their favorite pizza joints-as long as no one mentioned anything. Toys were handed out like the former and latter rains. The three children amassed fortunes, booty that they hoarded in basements, attics and bedrooms, under the eyes of "watchers" who occasionally came to pick them up from school, a grandmother here, a grandfather there.

While Flower got "better" and mainstreamed out of ABA therapy school into normal classes, Anukai's exhausted father hid out in the basement doing the laundry that his mother-in-law usually did so that his wife didn't have to.

"She is going to learn how much she really needs me when someone else is fucking appreciating me in her fucking face-they won't last without me."

He meditated darkly as he busted his ass for them anyway, like lashing out both at her and a world equally bent on his negation would erase the hell they all had just gone through, that he'd felt he'd gone through all by himself.

He had crumbled being the rock of the family and the haunted walls of his house never let him forget it. The veins that snaked along his temples throbbed as he looked for a way to make his wife see, knowing he'd leave before he let her drive him to either extreme his own parents had crashed through.

"I need to do it." he seethed to no one in particular. "Just to shut her up- to make her stop telling that bitch everything-" he snarled.

The last battle was over his right not to have his business out in the street versus her right to vent to her friends she clung to so ferociously that her desperate need for acceptance blinded her to the fact that all of them had slyly offered to satisfy him when she'd told them she couldn't soon as she was out of earshot. At company picnics, doing yard-work, even coming out of the store loaded down with groceries and their kids.

But Fern took the cake because she lived right next door and every chance she got she'd shoot her shot. Her grating voice erupted in his mind. "Seeing as though they've intensified with your lay-off...she was telling me all about it the other day."

"I need to do it," he growled, hurt that his wife had him out there like that. He slammed the dryer shut and pressed his hands against the vent that sent hot air out onto the driveway next door, too in his thoughts to notice Fern's car had just pulled in.

"No...what you need to do is find that wolf dog you promised your fucking kid and pay attention to what is going down in your own house." the basement walls whispered. If they hadn't been talking sense, he would have noticed that no one else was actually there with him to say it.

"Yeah, that's what I'll do- Maurice said his husky just had a litter..."

"SO... we doing this or what? Since you all backlogged- let's just do this while nobody's around-" Fern hissed into the vent, startling the father with her sudden presence up against the foundations of his house like a snake. She had bent down so that all he saw was her double chin and tits. Something in him snapped.

"Leave the back door open-" he muttered.
"But why not over there?" she started whining suggestively.

"I'm not fucking you in my house. Leave the back door open, bitch." The father snarled and walked away, leaving the basket of clothes on the floor as he put on the Mandingo mask his dad had left Alabama refusing to be, only to turn into up in Cleveland, too. Fern was left on her knees in the grass like the venomous viper she was, tingling over how ready and willing he was to openly disrespect her.

"That's alright," she muttered as she stood up and sashayed up her back porch and into the house, "fuck him and his attitude! And when this shit is over and done, all that shit she rubs in my face is gonna be mine!" she cackled to herself.

chapter fourteen

GrandPere was lost in his thoughts after that night's vigil at the church. It was their seventh night in a row, for the seventh month, seven years to the day the madness first broke out on top of the heroin epidemic that hadn't loosened its grip for more than a decade.

The ghetto they'd no other choice but to raise their kids in due to discrimination after migrating from the Caribbean for a better life had always been rough, but the crack epidemic turned it into a war zone. Parents watched in tears as their kids killed one another over control of the substance that made them forget the hellish maze they'd been born into for mere moments at a time.

Elders who'd survived World War Two, Jim Crow and the Civil Rights Movement had already watched their sons come home from fighting Charlie strung out if not in a box, and now witnessed their grandbabies getting mowed down by the same government-issued bullets.

Those still sleep found themselves lined up under preachers profiting from an Apocalypse Now mentality, organizing the weak to be fleeced of the little they had in the name of a Church that had sanctioned every bloodbath in modern history as eugenics, doling out a passivity as addictive as the smack and crack that the woke fought against in the trenches.

The awakened amongst the Greatest Generation reorganized like battalions in the basements of cloaked true churches, companies coming together in communion on Sundays.

They kept praying in platoons throughout the week against the blight their own children had been programmed to be upon themselves as they exterminated their own kind for the establishment, no assistance needed from the thin blue wall of silence whose slugs picked them off soon as they crossed out of the corners they'd been blitzed into.

His weary wife found his hand and pressed it to bring him back as they walked. She was still embarrassed by what had happened that night as they came together in fellowship with the Others. "The body does what it does," her husband whispered. "God sees what we cannot bear and makes moves he is not always inclined to share-"

"But the way they all looked at me-" she whispered back, her face hot.

"That was nothing but love, and concern- and confirmation. You didn't have to tell them you'd been crying all week. God told them because we're all connected by him-"
" But ...the way they said her name-"

"They saw our daughter's light as much as we did-" he murmured and kissed the woman on her crown.

The surge of intimate love steadied them after hours on their faces in the center of a circle of brothers and sisters that, without a word from them, got caught up into praying for the return of their child, one who had long ago been lost to the fires that burnt the streets above the basement they'd gathered in.

Restored, they walked home like warriors until the pins and needles hit as their stoop came into sight.

"I just hope she's alright-" she whispered.
"...Me too," he said hoarsely and kissed his wife on her forehead.

Suddenly the block reeked of sulphur as her third eye slashed open. The couple said a prayer, steeled themselves separately, then looked at each other. Spiritual armor rose up as they entered their own building.

chapter fifteen

Fire slowly danced down the red door frame, across black baseboards to the center of the cream carpet runner in the hallway. It pooled and made a slow but brazen bee-line to the mother and child one fiery footprint at a time.

About four yards from where the two exhausted bodies slept the flaming prints were stopped against their will. The demon roared at the mother and child peaceably asleep for the first time in forever. It pushed against whatever had stopped the reunion it so greedily desired after all this time.

It could smell the weakness on her, no different than when she was seven and rejected by the kids on the block because she was smart and shy. It recalled how many broken souls it had stalked her through as she'd timidly looked for love in the barren world outside her barred windows.

It blushed over how heady it had been. It had lurked for ages in the shadows, grazing her via hijacked humans with just enough cruelty to make her doubt her safety in the world before it found its base. The demon replayed it like a symphonic love affair instead of the twisted, pedophilic dirge that had been roaring out of the chest of the unassuming paper-pusher down the hall no one ever suspected. It had chuckled over finding the space he had moved into within the man already inhabited by demons more depraved than him and had instantly felt at home.

It had devoured everything it could within her upon first contact and cast her off when nothing was left, as demons tend to do. She had been its first decimation and held a strange place within where its angelic heart had been.

Delirious, the beast shook off the rhapsody, reared up and slammed towards the shell of its first feast. It was roughly flung back. It landed in a shocked, scattered heap of fire outside of the red front door its host lived behind.

The flaming demon careened wildly back down the hall then skidded to a stop, flames flying ahead of him as the elevator doors pinged open.

Two feeble looking old people slowly stepped out into the hall.

In a flash two masked, heavily armoured Guardian Angels blazed into the atmosphere right in front of them.

Terrified, the beast ran down the hall and dove for cover through the red door.

The first armored Angel followed and bashed the red door to bits in pursuit of the devil, a call to strike finally received that he'd waited an eternity for.

The other Angel turned to the grandparents of the newly dedicated child passed out on the floor with his prayed for mom. He scanned them to make sure they were okay.

The fully armoured spirits of the old couple stepped out of their shells and quickly pressed forearms with the second Avenger, who then followed the first down the hall after the demon.

chapter sixteen

The second Avenger found his cohort with his blade drawn as he loomed above the flaming devil, who'd cowered in a puddle of jizz at the pedophile's slack-jawwed, dozing, house-shoed feet. The only light in the living room came from a horrific photo montage of constrained little boys and girls that flickered as his screensaver next to his bottle of sugar spliced vodka and the still-smoking cigarette in an ashtray absently balanced on papers the man had brought home from work.

Incensed, the first Avenger to enter wordlessly took the flaming index finger of his sword-free hand, slowly dragged it down the curved ridge of his perfect nose and made a circle around the perimeter of the space with it, his eyes never leaving his prey. Other demons in residence who'd been waiting in the shadows popped out of hiding, pinned to the walls and doorjambs against their will.

The second Avenger winked, then clicked its glowing teeth at its cohort. They bumped free forearms before it growled and slammed the closest pinned devil of the domicile to the floorboards and roughly hacked its head off in front of the rest of them, laughing riotously as the beast's fellow demons cried out in protest.

The demon nearest him screeched about technicalities as he wildly lunged at the masked second Avenger who'd risen holding the head of the demon's comrade by the hair. "You can't DO that! Your Watcher class is not allowed to Interfere with the rules of the-"

The Avenger casually tossed down his bloody blade, pushed off its mask and violently threw it at the demon.

Uncloaked, Ulterior Angels popped into view alongside each of the tethered demonic beasts, blades and teeth bared.

"What the- You?! But you're- What do you have to do with what we get up to on this plane?!-" The technicality enamored demon screamed as the pod of Ulterior Angels viciously snuffed his co-horts out in his face.

A little of the light of the demon cowering at the feet of the sleeping pedophile who'd attacked Gabryl's mother as a child and gotten away with it dimmed as each demonic body hit the floor around him and was dragged off, officially and eternally cut from him like a pound of flesh one at at time. The second Avenger strode over to the first and held up its trophy, chuckling.

"Matched set?" he murmurred.
"Eh...why not?" The first Avenger grinned as he tossed his blade to the angel beside him, grabbed the smoldering demon by the throat and made its body bump into the table the cigarette and the vodka were balanced on. The room temperature alcohol spilled on the pedophile and woke him just in time to see the spirits of all the children he'd gotten away with molesting who had already perished gather around him.

Some had strung themselves out. Others had followed in his footsteps as if they'd been infected by a vampire. Still more had committed suicide. The souls of those still living had been pulled from wherever they were strung up as witnesses.

He looked up in shock as the two Avenging Angels popped into view pinning the head of the smoldering demon behind everything he'd done in his lap.

The child-sized spirit of the mother of Gabryl pushed through the cluster of fallen ones as one of the little boys materialized just enough to get a grip on the bottle he'd once been told was lemonade and passed it to her.

Her spirit fleshed out as she deliberately doused the night-terrored man with the remaining liquid before she gave the bottle back to the long lost spirit of James Morrison, the little boy who had been his first male victim.

Jimmy slammed the glass bottle into the pedophile's chest as two other children pressed their cold, dead hands into his face to muffle his screams the way he had muffled theirs.

Lil Danise, the mother of Gabryl, picked up the still burning cigarette and flicked it into her neighbor's chair then walked out, followed by the spirits of all the other ones also still somehow tethered to life, barely breathing in spite of all of the horrific things he had done as adults around them had looked the other way.

The Avenging Angels hacked the man and his favorite demon to bits as the chair burst into flames and the spirits of the children who'd already died finally floated up towards the highest high, flickering in the dark light.

chapter seventeen

"Danise! Gabryl!" The grandfather cried out and fell on his knees as he shook the two of them. His heart raced as he put his fingers against both of their necks and felt for their pulses.

"Baby!!- Oh-Dear Lord!!!" the Grandmother screeched as she lunged towards her filth- stained daughter, then fell back as the sight of her child holding her son in her gunk streaked junkie-arms cut her to the quick.

"Please God, No!" the grandmother wailed, " I always knew she'd wash up dead on our-"she cried out in fear.

"Watch your words!" The grandfather admonished his terrified wife. "We have to Speak Life! Even when it looks like death- Remember whose you Are!"

The grandmother cried "Baby, be okay- please be Okay- You.. .you are okay- Everything is okay-" her voice shook and fell away as somewhere deep within her she realized she was speaking truth.

"They're- they're breathing, baby-They're alive-" he whispered as his wife collapsed against him again on the floor in a heap. "Everything's gonna- gonna be- It's all gonna be okay." the old gentleman mumbled as he wiped the crud off his grown child's face. "She's- she's back from the dead and everything's-everything's gonna be okay this time- I can feel it-" The three generations remained sprawled on the floor in the hallway until Gabryl quietly came to.

"Grandma- Grandpere!" he cried out in shock and flung himself halfway out of his mothers embrace into theirs.

chapter eighteen

Pierce screamed like a struck animal and leapt from his recliner out of the nightmare.

His hand spastically fluttered at his sternum as bits and pieces of the terror evaporated in the early morning light.

He stumbled out of his slippers into his bathroom and wiped the spittle from his face in the warped mirror with barely a reflection. "It was just a dream, just a-" he muttered.

He splashed cold water on his face to wake himself. The hairs on his neck stood up in the silence that echoed around him. "...Hello?" he called out.

Nothing. He looked around, spooked.

"Whatever," he said nervously and turned on the shower before heading into his room to lay out the day's clothes on autopilot. He caught full sight of himself in the closet door mirror.

He saw himself without the beatific sheen of the demons he'd housed for years altering his vision for the first time and got sick to his stomach. "It was just ...games- and who cares? They were my...friends, we were just kids...just played- house...like kids do-" he said to himself aloud to shake himself out of it.

The room was silent where spiritually dark coddling usually all but clogged it. He warily snuck a peek at himself in the mirror, unable to escape the raw reality. He had not been a kid playing doctor with other kids for a very long time.

All his put-upon passivity vanished sans the support of the demons who'd encouraged him across decades of fucked up activity. The beast he'd already consciously chosen to become roared out of him.

"They wanted it-" he spat.

The meditations of his heart sans any devil around to sugarcoat it sung out like shots fired from a gun as he made his way to the kitchen and put on his coffee. "Served them right anyway... and- Parents ought to be ashamed of themselves. It's the parent's faults anyway. Who leaves their preciousness out in the open like that?"

He zigzagged across his apartment erratically as flashes of what he'd done to whom and where picked at the periphery of his vision.

"Parents didn't care about them- they never do- but I did- I saw their sweetness...smelled it- reveled in it-bathed with them in it when there was time- and I was always very kind to them in it- my little friends-" he huffed, deeply inhaling the scent of every decimation that went down in the apartment as it played across his memory, almost arousing him to a hunt he had given up with the times.

He beamed darkly back at the picture of unassuming passivity in the mirror in his room as he dressed without entering the still-running shower in the bathroom, deliriously proud because he'd picked himself up without the help of the demons for the first time.

"... I was the best thing that ever happened to each and every one of them..." He arrogantly muttered to himself as he tightened his perfectly tied tie.

The words echoed in the room, made him pause to look at himself in the mirror again.

His six year old self stepped out of him, brokenly stared up at the monster he had grown into and curled up at his feet. Just like Pierce used to do at his father's.

Adult Pierce flinched as the memories flooded back. The skin across his aroused groin began to violently itch, then his chest. He'd shielded his face from the fists that pummeled him until he was unconscious time and time again as a child so his father could force himself drunkenly on him, muttering the whole time.

"I'm the best thing that's ever happened to you, boy~"

Pierce clawed at his dress shirt roughly. Blood seeped through. He pulled his hand away in confusion, only to see shards of glass embedded into his bleeding fingertips. He ripped off his shirt as blood poured from the gash in his chest where the bottle had hit him in the nightmare, now viciously recalled in full detail. He blindly ran back into the living room. He saw chunks of glass scattered around his favorite chair for the first time.

"No! This can't be-" he hissed as the skin on his arms shriveled up as if burned. He blinked and the charred recliner smoldered in front of him. Pierce closed his eyes against the smoke for a split second only to open his eyes on his own drunken father roughly sodomizing a seven year old him with his face pressed into the Lazyboy he'd inherited upon the sick man's death many years ago. Pierce crumpled to the floor as the blocked memories of his father brutalizing him whirled around him.

Everywhere he looked he saw his acts of abuse against neighborhood children alongside the acts of violence against him as if they'd occurred at the same time. The fucked up spirit of his father had been beside him each and every time he had bitten down into an innocent to keep his own whited- out memories at bay, the cannibalistic mental infection passed on like a virus.

"That was why it felt like home- " Pierce whispered to a room with no demons to manipulate or conceal the truth.

His as violently beaten mother had only institutionalized the attacks. She'd called him a sick faggot for what she said he made his father do, then took solace in the boys screams for years after the fact. "It was Better you than always me, faggot... Who the fuck cares what happens to you anyway?"

That had been the last thing Pierce's mom had said to him on the day she delivered his inherited throne to him. She died shortly afterwards and Pierce had completely whitewashed every memory of his entire clan.

He broke down and cried, puking up years of the clear alcohol that his dad had forced him to drink as the abuse continued. He marveled at the sting of the sweet, clear liquid on the open wound in his chest, the first thing his suppressed heart had felt in forever. Pierce slowly crawled over to the land line and shakily called the office. He cleared his voice.

"Um, I'm running a little late today," he muttered flatly to whatever the response was on the other end of the line. "... No, no...I'm fine... but I'll be a little late."

Pierce lumbered into the now scalding shower and scrubbed himself raw under the hot water.

He slashed at his eyes until he was blind again, numb, temporarily safe from the recollection of it all, including his own consciously enacted crimes sans any memory to justify it on the surface.

chapter nineteen

Life went on and unspeakable things got buried.

The cherry and crab apple trees out back died from root rot as more latch key kids moved into the neighborhood, everyone's lower middle class parents working to cover mortgages on big, empty houses as whites moved to the suburbs in disgust.

"This is just as nice as there-" she whispered to herself unconvincingly as she played movie studio lot with her day-player doll cast of hundreds in the attic. "Okay... not Just as, but it is pretty cool," she purred.

Different scenarios went on all over the place like that MGM she'd read about in a Hollywood Babylon book found in one of the many old boxes of books her dad had picked up at Shaker yard sales. Keeping Anukai's jungles to the gardens around their house on that sun-stroked block took a lot out of her. She had abandoned the people of her universe for Dolls whose heads she could see over, toys bestowed on her and her siblings by parents so deep in their own trench warfare that they rained the gifts down on them as the only indication their children ever came to mind.

Anukai made her way over to the windows where the "sound-stages" for the romantic comedies were located and picked up where she had left off.

"Cut!" she cried and gave her notes on the scene to two of her favorite dolls featured in it. "I wonder what's the best way to shoot what's next?" she murmured then absently looked out the attic window at the two family house next door where her mom's best friend lived.

She blinked in confusion at her father in Fern's house, pinned under the fat thighs of the Mother's best friend just like his sister the Tsunga used to pin her.

Anukai convulsed and split into pieces. She stepped away from her selves. "...Too much goes down when I'm even... even a little bit away...but you..." she whispered to the part of her that was still crouched lovingly over the scene she was shooting, "you stay in here, and have fun-'

The part of her that was the best there was of her to her looked up at her questioningly. "...but is it safe?" All that she is asked. "I think so," Anukai shrugged.

"But why? No place else is-" her voice trailed off. "Somewhere has to be," Anukai whispered to her favorite part of herself. "And if it's not...I will blow everything apart-" a splinter said. "Ok- Don't forget where we-"
"I won't, I promise-" The thirds of her said in unison. They pinky swore and hugged.

Anukai played in the real world from that point onward.
She could smell the beast that stalked them in the house. Tides of tainted blood crushed against the foundations of her family home so loudly they became white noise to her day. Without her ever speaking on what she saw, within three years that felt like three days, the father was gone.

The big-footed wolf dog he'd gotten and left to protect Anukai howled for as long as she did, waiting for him to come back and get her like he'd promised he would.

chapter twenty

Gabryl and Danise stepped into the elevator hand in hand after a day of looking at dinosaurs and stars at the Natural History Museum and Planetarium. They both beamed, happy because they got to go do things together now that she was all the way there. They shyly yet utterly adored one another's company.

"I can't believe how much you know about Everything!" Gabryl crowed for the umpteenth time that day.
Danise blush-grinned down at her son. "Believe me, Gabryl...not Everything~"

"Yeah, but you know about the planets and eclipses, you even knew more about Pterodactyls than the lady giving the tour!" he sung out proudly.

"Yeah...I did used to love me some dinosaurs~" Danise grinned and ruffled Gabryl's hair. "Gabloomy~Where do you think you get it from, huh? Mr. Smartypants~?"

Gabryl blushed and looked at his toes as his way of seeing the world sung out of him due to the love in the elevator and made every button glow. He stuck his chest out because he was Smart... and it made sense because his momma was smart too.

We'll be dinosaur doctors together, he happily imagined to himself. In his mind's eye they instantly had clipboards and white coats on, and glasses, oohing and ahhing over huge discoveries in dinosaur bone slivers under microscopes. The elevator bell chimed and the doors opened onto their floor. Danise's hand tightened around his so sharply that Gabryl got pulled out of daydreams just in time to see his mom bare her teeth.

The color drained from Pierce's face as he jumped back in

alarm.

Gabryl's jaw dropped as he saw all the light in the elevator slam into his mom and make her glow as she pushed him behind her. Danise vehemently pointed at the shocked man who lived down the hall and flung her hand roughly away from her, casting whatever little bravado the craven man had retained away like it was a scrap of fabric.

Pierce awkwardly backed away from her before he turned and all but ran for the stairs at the other end of the hall.

"Mama, you Okay?" Gabryl whispered nervously into his dazed mother's coat.

She took a deep breath and released all the rage that had arisen at seeing her abuser as a sober adult for the first time.

Danise bent down so she could be eye to eye with Gabryl.

"Listen to me, Gabryl" Danise whispered. "That man- stay away from him, Okay? Will you promise me that? He's...very.. .very bad- I do not care what any adult tells you to do- You- do- Do not get in an elevator with him, do not take ...candy- Do not talk to him on the-" Danise wiped nervously at her nose.

"I won't, momma," Gabryl whispered and nervously wiped at the single tear that skidded down her cheek. "I promise I won't." he threw his arms around her neck then growled "Pick me up!" like a T-Rex into her hair.

"Ahhh Gabloomy~" she sniffed, steadying herself as he growled again.

"Wait a minute-" she did a double take. "You're- you're not my Gabloomy! You're-You're a a baby T-Rex!! Ahhh!Ohh No!!!" Danise sung out into the hallway.

"Yeah, but I'm a baby T-Rex so I'm harmless! Sooo Lift~!" Gabryl sang back.

"Okokok-" Danise scooped the son that was her sun up into her arms and carried him into her parent's home.

chapter twenty one

On the one- month anniversary of Anukai's Dad leaving the mother called her down into the kitchen.
"Sit down," the mother growled and pointed at a chair dragged into the center of the room. She had pushed the table and the rest of the chairs away so she'd have room to pace. Anukai looked warily over at her mother's mother who leaned against the stove, supporting her spoiled daughter in whatever she did, as usual.

Anukai took her seat, looked down at her hands and steeled herself against whatever they'd cooked up this time. It'd been open season ever since he'd left without her. The wolf dog's water had already been poisoned for trying to protect her.

"...You thought he loved you, didn't you?" the mother hissed. "Yeah, you pranced around here like this was more your house than mine due to him...like the World was your Oyster... and now he's gone...and-" She abruptly stopped. The memory of Anukai's telepathic threat from the backseat of the Monte Carlo years ago fluttered across her senses. Anukai looked up darkly through her brows above the head of the mother, silent on every channel. "And I am going to make YOU Pay-*for ALL of it*-" The mother snarled.

The mother's mother looked at her headstrong grandchild in disgust as the veil shifted slightly and spirits in the kitchen showed themselves to the child. The grandmother cleared her throat to steady her daughter so she'd have the strength to do what needed to be done. Children needed to remember their place, even if you had to bash them back into it every once in a while.

"I knew I was going to get to someday- I knew his flaky ass didn't give a fuck about anybody-not even his lil Nuk-" the mother choked as she spat out his nickname for the child.

Anukai said nothing, just watched through her knit brows as the dank spirits strung up between her mother and grandmother danced on the ceiling.

"You think he's coming back to get you like he *said* he would?! He's not coming back! You chose the wrong team and you're going to pay for it!" the mother screamed as she stormed in lopsided circles around the silent child. "You're nothing, you hear me?! I always told you that and your precious daddy finally showed he agreed with me! Nobody gives a fuck about you and never will!"

The grandmother cleared her throat and solemnly joined in on the barrage. "Nobody wants you, Anukai! You're a liar- saying all those nasty things about good people to your kindergarten teachers! I'll never forgive you for that... because THAT showed your Heart for this family! And You're ugly- with that nose just like that darkie she had you with, and nobody ever wanted you anyway- not even him! What did your nasty lil butt DO for his mean ass to be so nice to you anyway?! Probably the stuff you lied and said everybody else did- How else would you even know about those kind of-"

The grandmother sucked air roughly through her teeth before she lashed out again at the still silent, glowering child. "You Dirty little girl- I know- I can tell these things! I always knew something was wrong in this house-you nasty, nasty little girl-" the grandmother hissed.

"Mom!" the mother broke in to stop her.

"He wasn't- it wasn't anything like- with-he didn't do that with her!" she yelled then steadied herself. "Nobody wants you!

We're Stuck with you! WE- we have to feed you!"

Anukai sat motionless and watched less dark spirits look on sadly, all refusing to do anything to break the onslaught as the mother waved her arms wildly. Anukai swore to herself as a sixth finger on each of the mother's hands veered dangerously close to her face.

Emboldened by the sound, the two women stormed around the child like witches casting spells. "You'll be lucky if you eat anything at all!" The grandmother hissed, caught up in the spirit of things. "What? Aren't you going to cry? You usually do-only there's no one to hear you now! Oh, you poor, little filthy thing-"

The mother had often bragged about doctors cutting the extra fingers off when she was a baby. She remembered the librarian saying the best tell for tracking demons was six fingers and toes, like the ones on the giant skeletons found in mounds in the Ohio River Valley a few hours south of Cleveland. She'd seen the kid's perversely curious response to giant lore after being called Goliath for fighting back.

The bloodline marker was still on her mother in the spirit for any clairvoyant to see alongside all the other darkness she rolled with. Anukai sucked air through her teeth, bewildered and oddly relieved. Though carried, Anukai realized that maybe the mother was right all this time. She was not one of their kind, whatever they were.

The mother roared. "You think I have to spend MY money to make sure you eat? Mark my words-I'll watch you starve as I eat in your face!"

"Your precious Daddy doesn't give a fuck about you, you hear me? He's never coming back!" The mother's voice hitched in her throat as bewilderment at being left behind swarmed her as thickly as the venom she spewed surrounded her still somehow stoic daughter. "You think- you think you do all this! That it's Your story and we're just living in it! That You write your story-"

Her face darkened. "You don't write shit! You are here out of Fucking Necessity- I carried you to shut his Black ass up! So he wouldn't be shipped off to Vietnam like his fucked up cousin D when being in college wasn't enough! And Now I'm fucking stuck with you since he-" The mother paused, bewildered as the truth tumbled out of her. "I can't believe he finally did it- just gave Up and Left me..." she hissed, momentarily mystified, pulled away from the here and now. She shook it off and Anukai's ambivalent face came back into focus. "With you!" she snarled.

"YOU will survive only if I decide to let you! You'll be lucky if you make it out of here Alive!" the mother hissed as she shoved the chair. Anukai fell to the floor and looked up balefully as her grandmother leaned in and kissed her daughter tersely on the cheek.

"You'll be okay, baby," the grandmother whispered to her youngest daughter. "We don't get to choose the children we bear. Everyone can't be as lucky as I was when I got blessed with you." the grandmother purred at the mother, stroking her cheek proudly.

Wordlessly, Anukai stood up, solemnly sat back down in the chair and waited.

She stared sullenly down at her own hands as the diatribes reloaded. The more they attacked, the stiller she sat, waiting for them to tire themselves and the evil spirits on them out. The lines on her palms danced as her consciousness floated above them like a red tailed hawk in flight. She blinked and saw people she had once made from above, at peace with one another, unaware that she still cared for them no matter what hell surrounded her where she really was.

It made Anukai think about what a real God watching over things would be like in a way she rarely had space to and made light of the vicious attack she was under.

Anukai decided to note it all but not to listen to what she was hearing in Hell all the way, the same way she'd long ago decided not to see as much as she truly could. A twisted smile threatened to play across Anukai's lips right before the grandmother turned back around and cut her eyes at the child.

Exhausted due to the flow of hate from the seat of her soul, the grandmother gathered her things to go home and get ready for that evening's Jehovah Witness bible study.

The mother continued to mimic the litany of horrors the sheer beings around her spoon-fed her, trying to wound her daughter. By the time the mother was completely done, Anukai felt years older than she was and equipped to soldier through from then on out.

chapter twenty two

Gabryl stood beside his Grandpere's bed and peered into his ear. It was covered with the peach fuzz of old age, but Gabryl knew he was still in there, regardless of what everyone else said.

The aides whispered to one another as if neither he nor the usually catatonic, weak little boy was there. "When he comes to, he's just crazy!"
"Yea, it's better that he never does when they are here-" "It's for the best- that poor woman-"

"Such a horrible accident-and the factory is refusing to-" "Such a sad situation-"
"If it's anything like last time, God knows it's better if he never comes back to at all-" the lead nurse murmured.

Gabryl's head whipped up and he flew into a rage. "Don't Say That! Don't you dare Say that! Grand-pere! Don't listen to them! You evil old ladies! Stop trying to send him to hell! Get out!!" he screeched.

The women looked up in shock as he ran at them and chased them out the room, swinging. Panting, he locked the door. "Young man! You open this door right now!" the nurse's aide yelled, banging as he walked back to his grandfather's bedside, chest heaving.

"Don't listen to them, Grandpere- please!I- I need you here- don't go- Don't go... yet-" he cried out and gingerly laid his head on the old man's chest.

"Open this door right now, if you know what's good for you!" she seethed.

Gabryl narrowed his eyes as he blocked his ears, trying not to hear her.

"Open it or something bad is going to happen to-"

Wildly, Gabryl leapt up and violently slammed his entire body against the inside of the door, making the aides jump back in shock. He ripped it open.

"Something bad?!" he snarled and stepped towards them menacingly as they nervously inched down the hall. "Worse than this?! Worse than this?!" Gabryl screeched.

"I just heard you Pray that- God Take my Grandpere! You cursed him like I wasn't even there! You don't do that! Not to him!" he screamed. "You are supposed to care FOR him!" Gabryl pointed at the old man, "That's your job! Not to hope he dies! You want to wish Death on him?! I'll show you death! Get Out Or I'll kill both of you- you'll get to your God before HE does- GET OUT NOW!!" he roared, his little body drenched in sweat.

The women scurried to grab their purses and fled the apartment as Gabryl chased after them. He slammed the door behind them then stumbled back to his Grandpere's bed-side.

Distress was carved into the child's face so roughly that the old man fought against every tube in him to reach out. Finally he was able to make his left eye twitch.

Gabryl saw it and cried out hoarsely "Grandpere-?" The old man winked at the boy again.

"Hi-" Gabryl whispered heavily and broke down, crying all over the man's face. The child's tears sent shockwaves through the epidermis of the old man's skin and something deep within him connected and roared out. Gabryl felt him shake, but refused to let go. Suddenly the old man roughly turned his head and Gabryl felt the side of his face drawn to the old man's ear. He pressed his own ear to his Grandpere's ear and listened to the fight rearing back up in the old man against the pleurodynia like a wild symphony.

"Don't go yet- not yet-" Gabryl whispered. "I know you have to leave- just- not yet-"

Grandpere's voice boomed inside the little boy's head for the first time in his entire life. "...Okay, son-"

Gabryl leapt back a bit in shock and wrinkled his brow, mystified. His grandfather's chuckle wrapped around the inside of his head. "Hullo, son-" Gabryl gently shook his head in disbelief. "You're not going to say anything back?" The old man's spirit murmured.

"..Please don't go?" Gabryl hesitantly said aloud.
"Not- not out there...in here..." the old man whispered telepathically and laughed. The little boy wrinkled his nose into the sweetest smile the old man had ever seen and curled up in the bed around him.

"Hello~!" Gabryl giggled serenely as all the air went out of him in relief. They laid there murmuring softly to each other for what seemed like forever, drunk off the spiritual love that filled the room.

"You know you're gonna have to apologize to those eldercare church ladies, right?" Grandpere murmured in the spirit as his body remained unchanged.

"Ioneven Like church but even I know they were speaking the wrong way over you- I couldn't- I couldn't take no more-" Gabryl mumbled inside. 'How are we- doing this?" he asked shyly.

"I always figured you had my ear. Always singing to yourself when you think no one is listening." The old man whispered somewhat laboriously inside the little boy's head. "Pretty sure everything else sings to you too, right?" Gabryl nodded. "Know what it means?" Grandpere whispered. Gabryl shook his head no.

"It means... things may ...may get real hard for a while ...but.. .you are always going to be able...to hear the truth...above all else ... if you remember that...that you can hear This high.. .you're gonna be okay, son. You hear me?"

"Iont want you to go tho," Gabryl whispered.
"You've already been where I'm going, son. I sat beside your bed as you did- you were too small to recall- but what I see .. .when I'm not here now?...I remember seeing it around you..." the old man whispered psychically. "Still saw it in your eyes sometimes, when you used to come out your room, full, happy." Gabryl tilted his head as a strange light glinted off the mirror in the room.

"You are why I'm not afraid to go, son. I always was before you came to be with us here. You- you're like my angel ahead of time, son. And I'm always going to be able to be with you, long as you hold on to where only you know that you know how to get to, okay?" Grandpere whispered.

"Don't let anybody take that away from you, no matter what. Okay? Promise me-"

Gabryl nodded. He let his tears flow as he watched himself in the mirror. It shifted slightly, underscoring what his grandfather had said. He looked down at the old man.

"I Promise." he whispered. "But you promise me something too-promise you'll wait for your wife-to get ready..." Gabryl whispered. "At least before you say goodbye."

It took everything the old man had to slowly turn his face back towards the ceiling.

"I promise," he wheezed and fell asleep.

chapter twenty three

Anukai's maternal grandmother smiled to herself as blessed big brother Seal rushed out to catch his school-bus. Flower had been dropped off at her school by the mother on the way to work.

The wizened woman glared at Anukai as she chewed overcooked grits and eggs she'd made for herself for breakfast. The mother's hatred hung in the air like a noose the kid knew her Grandmother was waiting to string her up with, especially after Anukai had been kicked out of the old lady's Kingdom Hall the day before for asking pointed questions about their beliefs, embarrassing the woman in front of the Elders. Anukai smiled so sweetly at her grandmother that she almost made both of them sick.

She had already forgiven the old hag for joining in the mother's D-Day attacks. Clash of the Titans had aired and she saw the old shrews huddled over their cauldron trying to foretell a future they had no control of and something had clicked. She realized they openly hated her...and had to take care of her anyway. By their own admission they felt they Had to do it. "Because no one else wanted her" wasn't even thought about. Anukai twisted it into the old religious lady every chance she got, building a battlefield between the two every morning she came over to do the housewife work the mother refused to do.

"Can I have a-" Anukai started.
"No." the grandmother spat out simply, lowering her beautiful flat forehead as if she was about to charge the growth-spurting kid across the table.

It was on the grandmother that Anukai gauged the effect of getting bigger, using the short, duck-footed, wizened black china doll as her actual measuring stick.

"...Well, can I at least warm them back up?" Anukai purred. She tried not to giggle as her stoic grandmother geared up for the bloodbath on the brink of going down.

"I said, No," the grandmother growled and blinked her lidless eyes at the kid who somehow had ended up with her mouth, flat face and almond eyes when none of her own kids had. She was more than willing to tackle the child.

Anukai crawled up onto her knees in the chair, took out a hefty scoop of sugar and drizzled it on the cold grits with a huge grin on her face, eyes never leaving those of her grandmother.

"You're going to eat all of that sugar too! So wasteful! Maybe you'll die from diabetes-" the grandmother hissed.

"Well That doesn't sound very Jehovah Witness-y at all! That wasn't Holy- that was very mean~" Anukai bleated happily. "Besides, according to your people, if I do die, at least I get to go to Sheol, and won't have to come back to Hell Or deal with you people in so-called Paradise on Earth!" Anukai sang out to the grandmother. "I'll be sweet and dead and yall will have to finally leave me alone in my grave-"

The grandmother jumped at her. "You'll be dead a lot sooner than that- mocking my beliefs to my face-"

"You don't even believe that!" Anukai lilted as she ran around the table, "You're just mad at God for you know what... you gotta forgive God~" she guffawed as she dodged the old woman's infamous He-man grip.

"Go to school." they spat at the same time, facing off.

Anukai took off before the grandmother could change her mind, leaving the cold breakfast to be thrown away. As she charged out of the house to walk to school alone she ran smack dab into the surprise of her paternal Graindaddy, who got along with the Black-Mongolian woman as good as the little kid. "Graindaddy!" Anukai yelled joyously.

The maternal grandmother came to the front door warily to inspect the joyful trill that had exploded out of Anukai. She saw him and narrowed her eyes at the old man from the other side of the family.

They nodded at each other gruffly before the grandmother locked the door and went back into the house.

chapter twenty four

"It was a very good thing of you to do, apologizing like that," The eldest caretaker clucked as the others preened on the plastic covered couches and nibbled on the cookies his Grandmother had nudged him to serve with the tea and coffee as a peace offering after church.

"Yes, you were very rude to us-" another fussed as she held out her empty cup towards the child, expecting him to fill it. His mother and Grandmother looked on from the kitchen, trying not to laugh. Eventually the church lady helped herself to a little more on her own, furrowing her brow at the little boy missing his cue.

"It's just that...I love him...I just got so scared when you said those things -" he said sincerely.

"Well boy, we didn't mean it like that-" the eldest woman murmured. "We were just feeling sorry for your mom, and your grand-momma...and you-"

"We don't need you to feel sorry for us- We need you to help my granddaddy keep getting better." Gabryl grumbled sullenly. "You keep looking at it the wrong way- If you only look for the bad, how can you even see when he's had a good day?" the little boy fussed.

Gabryl's grandmother stepped towards the parlor but his mother placed a hand on her mom's arm.

Something had shifted within her when she came to in her old bed. Danise was rocked by memories of her tired Dad's still strong arms wrapped around her as he'd continuously sent up prayers of thanksgiving, openly crying over her return from the dead everyday, refusing to hide his tears of joy.

As she stood in the doorjamb she felt the sensation of his tears on her scalp that she'd felt every time she'd awakened to him braiding her washed hair out of the way. The matriarchs looked at each other. Understanding passed between them. Danise went in first.

"Oh, Danise! Honey! You look so good!" the church ladies cooed and crowded around her. She blushed under the pressure then shook it off, holding up her hand before any of them moved in to touch or hug her. Gabryl's grandmother quietly came into the room and he shyly went over to stand beside her. Danise looked back at her firstborn and her mom.

"Ladies, we so appreciate your ministering to my Daddy in this dark time...and...God's seen your heart, and we are eternally grateful- but-" Danise looked back at Gabryl and her mom again. "But...I'm going to take care of him from now on." Danise said softly.

"What?" The church ladies gasped. "You?"

"It's the least I can do...after all he's done for me- for all of us." Gabryl looked at his mom, then up at his grandmother, who rubbed his shoulders.

"Are you sure...you're strong enough to... after everything you've been through-"

"We'll be fine, Martha," grandmother assured them, then graciously ushered the church ladies out of their home.

chapter twenty five

Graindaddy offered his hand in order to escort Anukai the few blocks to school. She happily laced her fingers in his and they strolled down the street, chatting happily about the weather and why in hell on earth she had decided to wear all she'd pulled on for the day at once.

Color drained from Anukai's face as they got to an oak tree in front of house that a friend of hers used to live in.

A broken big wheel appeared out of nowhere and creaked to a stop in the grass. It shifted in a jagged semi-circle and the grass turned the color of blood as the dented plastic handles swung towards her like her friend was still riding it. Tire burns from the crash she tried her best not to see every time she walked past his house stung her eyes. Anukai froze.

Graindaddy wordlessly scooped her up and carried her past the house of the little boy who had been run over by his drunk father and dragged into the street as all his little friends looked on in confusion. Anukai pressed her forehead into the greying stubble on his cheek and smelled the toothpaste, menthol cigarettes, and brut cologne that was him to her with or without the gin. She knew he saw it too.

As if the shared vision of the big wheel had shaken it back up out of her, Anukai closed her eyes and began to whisper into his ear what Tsunga used to make her do to her when he was drunk on the porch.

Graindaddy leaned his face away from Anukai and really looked at her. Years of bleary memories ripped across his consciousness as things snapped into place that he had been too angrily inebriated to notice.

"I'll kill her-" Graindaddy whispered as his eyes went black with rage.

Something in Anukai's chest released in the first time in forever. She hung onto the promise in his livid eyes like a lifesaver she hadn't known she'd needed.

Anukai shifted uncomfortably until Graindaddy nodded, stopped hugging her and placed her back down onto the pavement. She grabbed the four fingers of his huge right hand, pressed her head into his side and they walked on.

She felt more protected than she'd ever felt in her entire life because she knew. One day his words would come true. They always did. Because of the Logos.

They spilled onto Martin Luther King Boulevard. Other neighborhood kids heading to school marched like ants to different tunes in the same direction.

chapter twenty six

Gabryl looked up at the white clouds that hung heavy in the ash gray sky.

He kissed his balled up fists and stole a look at his stoic grandmother seated at the head of the hole the casket had been lowered into before he and his little brother silently tossed two handfuls each of dirt onto it.

"See you soon," he whispered. His face was wet but he didn't care. His Grandpere's words danced inside his head even though he was gone.

"Only the strong have the courage to cry."

The boy knew without anyone having to tell him that Grandpere was a good man. But the turn-out at his funeral had shocked them all, even his now frail wife.

The sadness glistened on her like rain even though not a drop had fallen yet. Danise stood right beside her. Gabryl's mother had not only gotten better, she'd stayed better. As clear as she could, considering where she had been.

If you'd told anyone who had witnessed Danise in the gutter that it was *her* who became their rock as the family prepared for his passing no one would have believed it.

They didn't understand how much weight a person who crumbled on that squalid, drug littered path had been up against inside and out and had collapsed under, and never had to, really. A return from the dead was that rare in the war zone. But word of her Lazarus walk had spread.

Her strength had bloomed after her devil run out of hell with Gabryl in her arms. Gabryl had watched in awe as she'd grown even stronger doting on Grandpere as he faded away. He saw the sharp light sing out his mom where her shadow should have been and encircle his grandmother as ribbons of her mother's waning red and pink light danced down into the open grave.

Danise steadied her as people from the neighborhood, Grandpere's work and two churches streamed pass and offered their condolences. He was no longer afraid of the Angels he saw sandwiched in the crush between them because Grandpere had explained they were part of the songs the two of them were somehow able to see, and their greatest gift. So overwhelmed were all in attendance by the strength and gratitude that beamed out of Danise's eyes that everyone overlooked her inability to bear offered hugs.

Gabryl peered into the press of faces shyly, like he expected Grandpere's face to be found glowing among them even though he knew he was really gone. His eyes kept being drawn to the dark, dejected countenance of the slight man who lived down the hall who had showed up on the edge of the crowd a little while ago and seemed to inch closer every step he could. Remembering the elevator incident, Gabryl watched in shock as the slight paper-pusher made his way to his mother and reached out as if to touch her from behind, his face darker with every breath. Instinctively, he protectively cried out. "Momma!"

Danise looked up in alarm at the sound of her son and whirled around right before Pierce made contact.

"Get AWAY FROM ME!" Danise screamed as she stumbled backwards against her mother.

"Baby- what's wrong?" Gabryl's grandmother cried out over

the stunned din that spread through the crowd. "What's going on?" she snapped out of her mourning and grabbed her shaking daughter.

"Why are you here?!" Danise roared, "Haven't you done enough to this family?!"

"Danise-" Pierce whispered, the wind knocked out of him by her ferociousness. He crumbled at her feet "I'm- so- so- sorry!" he choked.

"Get away from my Family!!!!" Danise screeched and kicked at him as members of the churches pressed towards them. An alarmed yet dignified church lady openly rebuked her.

"Danise!!-That is no way to treat this most respected man who came to pay respects at your father's funeral! How Shameful! And in front of your boys?! He is a tithing member of our church family and you will pay respect where it's due-"

"HE RAPED ME! AS A CHILD! He RAPED ME!" Danise exploded. "And I wasn't the only one, either! And You want to tell me how to treat his ass showing up at MY Father's funeral, Mother Rogers?! He molested every damn kid on the block you church ladies turned your nose up at! Yeah- everyone who ended up drugged out like Me!" she hissed, her face twisted up in rage as the crowd yelled in horror.

"How dare you!" Mother Rogers clucked her tongue as she wedged between an enraged Danise and a cowering Pierce, more indignant over the tone of what was said than the content.

"You never said any such thing to me about anyone-"

"You know what your old pastor husband did whenever any of us told on him, you spiteful old witch?!" Danise hissed, "He said they had to forgive him!"

"That's what the LORD says to do, you stupid child!" Mother Rogers huffed arrogantly. "If you'd spent more time in church You would Know the Faith-"

"Oh! But that wasn't it!! If only that had fucking been it!" Danise yelled at Mother Rogers and lunged at Pierce, her mother refusing to let her go.

Danise shook her mother off of her. "I'm sorry, momma-" she whispered. "I should've told you...somebody- but-" The guilt and shame of not saying anything after seeing how adults had responded to others crept up on her but she knocked it away defiantly."I have to do this-"

"I'm saying it now- for everyone who can't-" she said valiantly and steadied herself against the judgmental barrage of insults pelting her from the church elders of the congregation Pierce belonged to.

"You're Lying!" Mother Rogers snapped authoritatively. "You better go into your prayer closet and pray God doesn't strike your lying-"

"They are why you and daddy Left that damned church... after what happened to Gabloom when I was already gone-" Danise whispered and found her frozen son's eyes in the crush. Released, he and his little brother ran over to her and his grandmother in shock.

"You're a liar!" Mrs. Rogers hissed again. Danise turned around.

"Want your congregation to know what he did next, Earla? Huh? ...I'm sure they'd Love to hear this-" she snarled and continued without letting Mother Rogers interrupt.

"A little while after each kid told Their fucking Pastor...a lil while After he told each CHILD who told on Mr. Pierce to forgive this DISGUSTING Fuck you're so ready to defend AT MY FATHER'S FUNERAL THAT HE HAD THE AUDACITY TO SHOW UP To After having RAPED me as a Seven Year Old Child ... because he gave your fucking church 10% of what he made...Your husband- Your FUCKING Man of God-You know...the one who was fucking every piece of barely legal ass that got entrusted to him for counseling as you looked the other way and dusted your fucking hats?! Your supposed Man of God -HE tried to molest them too!"

"You are Not going to-" Mother Rogers hissed but Danise kept going.

"And the ones who didn't believe his lie that it was okay? He told them that no one would believe them over him if they said a word! That God let it happen because they were damaged goods! Imagine hearing THAT as a kid...from your fucking pastor...as he's fucking molesting you! THAT is why I never told. That's why NO one said any such thing to You about shit-"

"You are nothing but a drugged up, used up lying whore!" Mrs. Rogers bellowed. "How dare you! How dare you?!"

" You will NOT besmirch the glorious name of my dearly departed husband with some twisted crack-head fantasy -a ridiculous, smacked out fever-dream- whatever the fuck your drug of choice is-"

The church members gasped at Mother Rogers use of profanity. "Where are your other victims, huh?! Since you're spreading this nonsense- at your own father's funeral no less, in your poor mother's face- in front of all these sanctified people! You

Dare insult my dearly departed husband's name now that he's not here to defend himself?! He's seated at the right hand of the Lord in Heaven, Witnessing you lie on him-"

"The only Lord your fucked up husband is sitting beside is the Lord of the Flies!" Danise hissed. "And he's on his fucking knees- Like he used to force the kids to be-"

The crowd gasped.

"Every kid his fucked up actions sent to hell ahead of him due to overdoses is bashing his fucking face in every single day as their closest semblance to heaven possible!" Danise snarled.

The members of the sanctified congregation of "*Many blessings, Giveth and Taketh away*" howled in outrage at the blasphemous accusations spewing from Danise.

The Others from the church her parents had found refuge in after being failed by Giveth and Taketh Away streamed through the crush to encircle the grieving family as actual Angels in the crowd wedged between the camps.

"Eddie Monroe. Jacinta Thompson. Precious Smith. Roberta Marks. Ricardo Jones-" she screamed in a raw, staccato voice over the melee.

Danise stood rigidly yelling the names of the children she'd known Pierce and the Pastor to have attacked, most whom had gone on to die of overdoses.

"Stop her! She's lying!" Mother Rogers yelled. Everything in the graveyard got quiet as a hot, empty Tuesday in July even though it was packed to the gills, except Danise.She continued to roar .

"Takeisha Reynolds. Karina Clarkson. Maddy Williams. Ebony

Willis. Ronald Mayweather, Anton Crusher- Half your church's fucking praise and worship department! He Made pedophiles out of as many spirits as he fucking broke- He even pointed And fucking provided some of them with their first tastes of heroin to ease their pain, shit that eventually they saw as their only fucking way out-"

"You better dive back into your crack den with this shit, you fucking addict-" Mother Rogers heaved. "This is slander! This is Blasphemy! I need to call the cops! I need to call on God to strike your filthy ass down right now! Lying on my chaste and dignified Husband! How dare-"

"Robert Murphy, Kenneth Downton, Ricky Jenkins- Dead! Dead! Dead!-"

Danise stopped in the middle of her roll-call and tilted her head as if God himself was whispering in her ear.

The softness that spread across her face made the venomous words loading in Earla Rogers mouth from the truth of her heart skid to a stop.

"OMG-You...Knew! Oh my God- and all this ...all this time, I-" Danise whispered aloud then started to laugh.

"You were complicit! You Knew what he was doing to kids too, and just didn't care- Just like In the name of whatever demonic Lord he actually served you never cared about the ladies in your congregation he was fucking-"

The entire crowded gasped over how cavalier Danise said the one thing they all already knew.

Mother Rogers could care less about what the one who made all the females in his flock call him daddy did as long as he was referred to as Pastor and she was positioned as Pastor's wife.

Her tawny skin went white with rage, her speechless mouth flapping in the wind as her own congregation awkwardly turned towards the truth.

"So you know what, Mrs. Pastor's Wife, Earla Rogers?" Danise hissed. "The blood your husband ordained to keep being spilled amongst the most vulnerable in yall's flock? Blood that eventually spilled into the gutters of these streets due to the monsters he was in League with? In the name of Jesus... that all can now see you in no way or shape serve no matter how you preen on a plush throne behind an altar you all paid for from the money you got from your still impoverished, never bettered by your leadership ...flock~?"

 Danise growled " That blood burden is now officially transferred to You."

Mother Rogers started to protest.

"And it's witnessed not by just two or more, but all of these people present that Are in the body of christ-" Danise snapped. "And it'd be better for you to have a fucking rock chained around your fucking neck before you got tossed into the fucking ocean than to face what God has in store for you after all the innocence YOUR husband and YOU are guilty of destroying-"

The congregation of Giveth and Taketh Away roared, ready to riot. As Pierce stood up nervously their eyes flashed with sanctimonious rage.

"She's telling the truth." he yelled over the din.

Danise's mother grabbed back onto her child and held on with all her might as the elders from the Giveth and Taketh congregation flew back in shock, as if a bomb had gone off with his admission of guilt. The clouds broke and the rains finally came.

"About ...what I did...and what her," he motioned absently towards Mother Rogers, " What her husband...knew and did too. And I am so sorry-I- But it- it happened to me as a kid-" he said hoarsely, "and I just blocked it out-" he stopped himself. "No! Because that's no- It's no excuse!" he cried out and ran out of the graveyard hounded by outside knowledge of his dirty deeds in broad daylight.

The throng of funeral goers erupted then scattered.

chapter twenty seven

Kahn the younger smiled cockily up from the floor as he faced off again with Apoc, Apogee and Apex. "I was sure Third said.. .*Rekindle* the Fire." he murmured, "not snuff it-"

Apoc landed a swift kick to his former leader's now slight form. "Snap out of it, boss~"he growled.

Kahn the younger laughed "What is there to snap out of? I feel great!" he roared playfully " And look at me- Look at this beautiful visage- I mean- look at me... I am one beautiful, albino motha-"

"I always forget how obnoxious you are when you are close to coming back online, Sir-" Apogee groused, not hiding her aggravation as she slapped him silly. He went flying.

"Don't call me Sir," he wheezed.
"Come on, Boss, gotta get used to it again!" Apex chortled as he helped Kahn to his feet, sucker-punched him and dropped him back onto the floor in a heap.

Globyl looked on impassively as Mohawk and Trini stood beside her, bemusedly taking in the beat down."Every time?" Trini muttered in disbelief.

"It's the only thing that works. It's like he's underwater or something."
"Mustabeen a true ahssehole, spirt'ly speaking-" Trini chuckled.

"Worst of the worst...Occasionally, yes-" Globyl laughed as Apex helped his old leader back onto his feet again and swung at his breadbasket. Kahn deftly blocked him.

"Stop...Doing that~" Kahn grunted and glared but still smiled.

"Nope-" Apex sang out. He sacked Kahn like a bushel of peanuts. "Not until you rise all the way back-oof!"

Apex took a knee to the groin as Kahn flipped him off ofhim and growled.

"Apologies, Sir," Apogee murmured against his ear as she wrapped him up in a sleeper hold.

"Fuck-"Kahn the Younger whispered before quickly reaching back, ducking out of the hold and flinging her at the feet of Globyl and the two freed women slowly adjusting to what the afterlife in service of the Third head of council entailed.

"Better!" Globyl cheered raucously.

Apogee growled as the freedwomen hooted and Kahn the younger bowed in deference to their applause. She darted over and slammed him back into the sleeper hold, lowering him gently to the ground.

"Grow up, Sir~" Apogee muttered as the lights began to go out for Kahn the Younger.

The trio of Globyl and the Freeds moved on.

Apogee hissed"You're such a lil fuck as a teenager-Ow! Son of a-!!"

chapter twenty eight

They rode on in silence.

The grandmother held Danise's head as Danise wrapped all of herself around her two shaken, solemn boys. Finally she spoke.

"...All this time-why didn't- you tell us? Why didn't you tell me?!" she whispered against her daughter's face. "Why didn't you tell me That was it-? I asked you so many times to just tell me what was wrong- to tell me what was going on with you!"

"I know mama, I'm sorry-" Danise whispered, crying softly as the taxi pulled up in front of the center.

They went in to drop Gabryl's little brother off in silence, soaked through with sadness. He started to cry when they tried to leave.

"Mama, I-" Danise started hesitantly." What a horrible way to let Pere- I ruined-"

The rest of the funeral had gone on after the congregants of Giveth and Taketh ran away in the rain. Danise had crumbled under the weight of the eyes of all those who hadn't left, who stood in silent solidarity with her family in ways she had finally started to understand that afternoon.

She had achingly let herself be hugged, hearing every word of encouragement the God-filled elders her parents had found themselves amongst after breaking away from Giveth and Taketh away spoke over her in their hearts.

Danise's mother grabbed her daughter by the face. "I'm fine, baby - And Pere was there, proud of you for speaking the truth! It was the perfect send-off, seeing his baby free herself from everything that he'd watched squeeze the life out of you all these years! You ruined Nothing, understand? But you gotta tell me...Are You okay right now?"

Danise looked down at the floor, then into her mother's grief-scarred eyes. "No...but I will be alright. Carried all that for so long...surely speaking on it won't be the thing that's the end of me, right? Though I walk in the shadows of the valley of death, I will fear no evil, right?" she sighed, unintentionally inverting the actual scripture as the little boy born with issues due to her addictions squirmed in her arms.

Danise kissed her youngest on the face again and again until he calmed down. She asked the attendant if it was okay if she stayed and tucked her special needs son in that night like she used to. The attendant on duty looked over his shoulder and nodded. Her victory over her demons had been one of his proudest moments.

"I'll take Gabryl home, baby- you take care of him...and hurry home, okay?" Gabryl's grandmother whispered. Danise nodded woodenly.

Gabryl bear-hugged his brave mother and T-Rex growled into her neck. "Be okay, ok mama?" he whispered, his voice quaking because he had seen that wooden look on her before, whenever she took him into the piles.

"I love you Gabloomy," she growled. "I love you too," he whispered.

Gabryl looked back at her from the door and got struck with the fear that he'd never see her or his little brother again. He cried out in shock and charged them.

"Promise me, momma- Promise me you are gonna Be Okay!"

he cried out and leaped on his mother. "You have to stay! You have to stay- I can't-" he whispered roughly "I can't be here without you-"

"Baby...I promise you. Dino Doctors honor," she murmured as tears streamed down her face.

They huddled there, what was left of the family hugging each other for what felt like forever.

Gabryl kissed his little brother three times on the face, kissed his mom even more, then finally they parted ways.

chapter twenty nine

"Umm...Marok, Anad, Yr-is and Soigné -" Hezuz called out. "A little help ?"

"Your turn," Marok muttered at Yris.
"Aw come on! Please! One of - I'll- Let's cast lots for-" Yris fussed.

Anad chuckled. " You must really be desperate-" "What does that mean?" Yris huffed.

"You lose at lots. All the time. Every single-" Soigné crowed as a trussed up Hezuz's whine echoed in the background.

"I do Not!" Yris exclaimed.
"We're in the highest High-It's your turn- lots are just

going to confirm it is-" Marok muttered and settled back onto his settee.

"Marok, Anad, Yr-is and Soigné ~" Hezuz sang out regally.
"It's like he sees us as one unit-" Anad snarked.

"He'd burst into flames if he had to say only one of our names-" Soigné hooted.

"When is this over?" Yris sighed.
"Third only knows, but we're one step closer to it if you just go and-" Anad chuckled.

"Fine- fine-" Yris muttered and sauntered into the vestibule as Globyl, Mohawk and Trini pressed in from the far side of Hezuz's temporary quarters, disgust on their faces from all they'd seen in the Almost- Eloh zone they'd had to pass through before coming to see the reason for all of its dogmatic, misogynistic depravity.

The four women nodded at each other as Globyl and the freed women followed behind Yris.

Hezuz sat motionless, huddled at the foot of a golden spiked throne. His body was coated in froth that immobilized him as it ate away at his rarefied, dead flesh.

"Refinishing the Kouros in preparation for release to the other members of Tryage," Yris murmured absently. Globyl and the Freed women nodded.

"I...think... I think I might actually be feeling this-" he laughed, teeth chattering.

"You don't...feel anything." all four women said in unison, irked by the haughty, bored clip his voice always seemed soaked in. Yris picked up the hose and roughly shot water at the crust of the solution coating him as he whimpered and whined like a dog through the ordeal.

When he finally was able to stand he glowed gloriously, brighter than the gleaming spikes on his interim throne. Hezuz plopped down on it like a barbarian king and slung his leg open over the arm of it suggestively, just to be a royal affront to the ethereal beings present he'd been entrusted to after escaping Puryf.

Ambivalent to the visual insult, Mohawk muttered "You seem to have missed a spot."
"Ah yes, a very Small one~" Trini concurred.
"Oh, you're right!" Yris exclaimed.

Before Hezuz could think to protectively close his legs the rough stream from the hose slammed into his groin and toppled him off of his temporary seat of power.

chapter thirty

Gabryl sat with his grandmother for the longest time as they waited for his mom to return.

Tears slid down his grandmother's face as Gabryl woke her up around 2am. He led her to her bed and tucked her in the way he'd watched his mom tuck in her dad the last few months. His grandmother stroked his sad, cherubic face and fell instantly asleep.

Gabryl stood there and stared at her for the longest time before he leaned in and kissed her cheek. "It's gonna be okay- we-we're gonna be...fine-" his voice cracked.

Sullenly, he made the rounds, making sure the door and all the windows were locked just like he'd seen Grandpere do. It was his job now.

He made his way into the room Grandpere had peaceably passed in and locked the door before he crawled into bed. Gabryl hugged the pillow and stared at the wall, refusing to come out until his mother came home.

After three days of his grandmother pleading with him from the other side of the door he finally heard her leave the apartment.

The elevator bell faintly chimed. Gabryl counted to himself the way he always did as if he was in the elevator with her, counted the speed of her shuffle out the building's lobby then exhaled harshly when he was sure she was gone. His shoulders shook against his will as he submerged himself in the feeling that everyone had abandoned him once and for all.

Gabryl caught sight of himself in the mirror hunched over in the middle of the room and got furious with himself over the tears that were trying to erupt when he knew with every fiber of his being that he needed to be strong.

"Stop crying- you can't- cry!" he screamed at himself in the mirror as his heart broke. He began to sob convulsively. Enraged, he wildly he lunged at his reflection as if he were going to smash it.

"Only the strong have the courage to cry" echoed in the air around him.

He momentarily forgot who, what or where he was, then just as suddenly remember everything.

...About her.

Gabryl dragged his forearm across his wet face, inhaled roughly and threw himself through the mirror in search of Anukai.

chapter thirty one

Out of the corner of his eye, Graindaddy noticed heat waves rising off the street like it was twenty degrees warmer than it was on this mild morning.

Graindaddy blinked as a cagey little boy with flashing eyes popped into focus. His Spiderman tee and dirty jeans spun into view before the rest of his features did as the boulevard began to morph into the dusty bank of a stream in the old man's mind's eye. Anukai stoically looked straight ahead.

The little boy trudged along the far side of the road as he looked hopefully over at little Anukai. Tears flooded out of his eyes between flashes of white. Anukai steeled herself and continued to walk forward as her left hand tightened around Graindaddy's fingers like a vice grip. Graindaddy cleared his throat.

"I think there's somebody here to see you-" he started.
"No there's not!" Anukai chirped back, cutting him off as she narrowed her eyes to focus on what was ahead instead of what was shape-shifting beside her.

"Come on, child, he- he looks like he's crying-" Graindaddy whispered reproachfully.

"Nobody's-" Anukai chirped with hollow happiness, "there, See?" she sang out and spun around as if she were looking at him. "I don't see anything- neither does anybody else. I'm just like everybody else. I don't see things! Especially not him-" she wheezed happily.

Gabryl flinched. His head hung low as he dug his fists into his pockets.

The family that he made out of twist-ties and let live in his pocket scratched against his knuckles as affectionately as wire and pressed paper could, reassuring him to call out to her again, that maybe this time it would work.

"Well, I see him." Graindaddy stated plainly and came to a stop. She stuck her bottom lip out as she tugged at Graindaddy's arm in vain.

"Well...you drink," Anukai whispered precociously. Graindaddy coughed in surprise and growled, then grinned. She growled back at him. "...well, you do."

"I drink so as not to see real little boys coming through just like that-" Graindaddy growled "So apparently I didn't drink too much-"

"Maybe I need to drink too, then-" she sassed.
"Anukai!" Graindaddy swatted at her.
"Fine-" She sighed and glared balefully over at Gabryl and acknowledged his presence. When she saw his wet face, her eyes dropped down to his chest. Before her spirit could make her ask what was wrong Anukai stormed off. Her grandfather strode to catch up with her.

"That was...very mean, little girl." Graindaddy admonished her."He may never forget that."

"He's not real anyway! And I'm not crazy! I can't see what other people can't see! I'm tired of seeing more than everybody! I wish my eyes would just-" Anukai screamed, overwhelmed.

She crashed into his legs and fought against the tide of tears rising in her chest. He bent down and hugged her.

"I understand," he whispered, remembering how crazy he'd felt before anybody told him as a kid what it was. "It's not pleasant, it's lonely...and you never know if what you see is for you or against you at first - that's a bad feeling, even when you get bigger-"

"Every time I go away to where- I know him from, bad things just- Graindaddy, he can't Be real-" Anukai whimpered.

"You better hope not-" Graindaddy muttered, "But unfortunately, things that come through like that usually are, one way or another."

He sighed. "Look-You're not crazy. It is a gift...but from who .. .is gonna be up to you in the end."

He locked eyes with his grand-daughter, still reeling from what she'd revealed about his own twisted youngest child, now twenty- one at least. He put it in the lead box in his head to deal with later, put a genuine smile on his face and placed both of his giant hands on Anukai's shoulders. "You okay?" he asked. She nodded. "You sure?"

The two of them crossed the street to the schoolyard. Graindaddy bent down and kissed her on the nose and then stood back up to his full stature and looked over at the spirit of the little boy and shook his head.

Hurt, Gabryl looked at Anukai and her grandfather, who he could tell saw him plain as day just like he knew she did. He dug his hands even deeper into the wire-paper people in his pocket and howled.

"Come back!" he screamed.

Anukai and Graindaddy slammed their hands over their ears as people trailed past them into the school's courtyard, oblivious to the shrieking around them.

Graindaddy gave her a second peck on her forehead. "Promise me next time you'll speak."he whispered.

Anukai grunted in agreement as Graindaddy pressed the third and final benediction of the day on her cheek, then turned and walked away as Gabryl screamed hysterically on the other side of the river until his voice gave out.

chapter thirty two

Deep within the valley of corpses she had wandered into, Gabryl's mother looked up.

That he'd survived to see three and a half after what he'd been born in and addicted to had been nothing but God. That she'd listened and had asked to put him to bed that night was too. But when she couldn't leave...feeling death breathing down her neck as he took his last breaths, she knew what she had to go do.

At 639pm, as she'd sat there rocking her weak baby boy in her arms, two hours after Gabryl and her mom had left the center, the heart of her youngest child had quietly gone out.

Danise struggled to remember how to dig but knew she had to lay her youngest son to rest as quickly as possible. She curled up on the ashen stomach of her child and sobbed until every thing was gone, baptizing him with her tears. She kissed his little caterpillar brows one last time and gingerly pushed black dirt over him in a place where everything else was left to dry rot in the open.

Her head whipped up at the sound of the screams of the son she had left ripping across the horizon. Her ears bled as she took off her necklace with pictures of them all in a locket, dropped it into the dirt and crawled deeper into the shadows of the valley of death.

Exhausted, an eternity later Danise curled up in a ball. The demons that had welcomed her back and danced mockingly behind her as she'd carried the spiritual body of her youngest child swarmed her, affectionately cursing her for having stayed away so long.

" Your Gabloomy is doomed, by the way-" the one who helped her prepare the syringe whispered nonchalantly. "You know that,right? May as well be already dead, too-" it laughed. "Everyone you love will be here soon, one way or another."

"God, forgive me for ruining the children you entrusted me with." Danise whispered wearily and slammed the plunger into a second triple dose of her medicine. She had been clean for years.

"...almost to the day." she mused and deftly prepared a third triple batch before the first she had gained entry on wore off. Gabryl's screams in the spirit were the sound her heart gave out to, rigor-mortised hand gripping the last loaded syringe.

A head demon pushed up through the second line of demons that had been trailing behind her. He sniffed at the soul he'd lost and found, victorious. He stood up, roughly lifted her broken body overhead and threw it to the ground, roaring as his minions cheered him on.

The frenzied crowd her discovery back in the valley of the dead triggered parted. Stairs appeared, bannistered by the fires of the region blooming along them. The demon dragged her corpse up by an arm he'd dislocated, head held high as he marched to the throne room of her heart. His minions followed behind, chattering joyfully. It took a moment for him to realize the pomp and circumstance he'd been expecting was not afoot anywhere else but inside his demonic mind and his trailing, tinny minions.

He looked around at the throne room it all had been for. It was utterly devoid of any activity. The demon roared in protest, throwing her corpse at the foot of the sovereign seat.

"Do Not HIDE from me!" The demon roared. His howls broke the stained glass from all of the lancet windows circling the space. "THIS is my kingdom now! I HAVE DOMINION! OVER ALL OF YOU! Show yourselves!"

A gust of cold wind rose up from the floor of the throne room and charged out of the broken windows, snuffing out every flame in the valley.

"What the-" the minions gasped as their fires died.
The spirit child of Danise stepped from behind the throne.

She kissed her stiffening adult self on the forehead then ferociously stomped on her wrist to make her hand release the syringe. Lil Danise turned around to face the demon she knew better than she'd known herself and leapt upon the beast, jabbing the syringe in the demon's neck.

"There's no one here left for you to rule, Demon-" she hissed. "Here's some of your own shit for the ride!"

The demon crashed to his knees in defeat, unable to muster more than a paltry wail of surprised protest. His shocked minions backed away as the child climbed off their overseer, grabbed him by the hair and peered into his eyes.

"I'm ....sorry-" the demon blubbered.
"I forgive you-" Lil Danise whispered tersely.

"What?!" The minions screamed as their leader writhed on the floor of the throne room, shrieking as he withered before their eyes, as if the child had spit acid on him.

Her forgiveness made him burst into black, sparkly sand.

The minions screamed and pushed violently against one another as they ran down the processional stairs they'd followed him up. Danise ran after them, savagely bellowing her forgiveness after them all.

Demons exploded left and right as her forgiveness of them

seeped through their crazed, anguished howls. Everything they'd corrupted turned to blackened dust.

For the longest time Lil Danise stood on an outcropping and watched as the black sand that was all that remained of those who'd tortured her forever got blown into the sea by holy winds that had kicked up out of nowhere.

The black sand beaches in the realm would forever be a reminder of demons finally fully felled by the only thing that truly worked against them after you'd done all you could do to stand: Forgiveness.

Eventually, she walked back up the stairs to the throne room.

She solemnly crouched next to the corpse of her adult self and kissed her on the eyelid. "I'm ok now. Thank you for coming back so we could finish it. Now go home...and never come back here again-"

chapter thirty three

Anukai was too riled to go into school just yet. She made her way across the lawn to sit under the malnourished cherry tree near the windows of her own classroom to wait for the bell.

She absently drew the characters for happiness she'd learned from her Chinese scrolls class at the art museum in the dirt and tried not to let her blinks draw out, knowing that to do so would call Gabryl closer. She didn't want to see him anymore since nobody else saw him and she was deciding not to be crazy anymore, like most kids did at her age when it came to invisible friends and special places. It was as a lone cherry blossom coasted down from above that it fully sunk in that her Graindaddy had seen Gabryl too.

Anukai gasped in shock as her head snapped up. Gabryl was crouched in the grass right next to her, silent, tracks of tears still streaked down his face because he was unafraid to cry around her. It had taken him forever to find her. He blew a spit bubble at her sheepishly.

She hesitated, then blew one back at him morosely. She sighed and wiped at his face almost defiantly, her little heart throbbing in her chest. The classmates who had rejected her for being bigger, smarter and younger than them streamed past as she played by herself, as usual.

The grassy knoll turned into a salty bay of tears that Anukai and Gabryl sat on the edge of. Rotting stumps of wood rose out of the water like old impaling rods dancing down underwater roads to kingdoms long since forgotten.

"I'm real." he whispered hoarsely.

"No you're not-" she sighed helplessly.

"Yes I am-you'll see! I am real- I'm here- just not here- but I need you to come back so we can- be able to- later- because- and it took me forever to find you-" Gabryl fumbled through the words he had practiced on his pillow, focused on those particular words since the news of the death of his little brother at the center the same night they'd planted Grandpere and his mom had disappeared again.

Words for Anukai blocked out the rattling in his grandmother's lungs as she moved, slept and wept her way through every day in the absence of her beloved, her daughter and other grandson. It was a rattle he heard through the walls, knowing that soon she would be gone too, leaving him alone. Anukai was the only actual love he somehow knew he still had.

"He saw me-" Gabryl pointed out hollowly."Was that your-" ".. .Graindaddy-" Anukai whispered sadly. "But he's weird too."

"At least you have him-mines- mine left-" Gabryl broke down beside Anukai in the dirt.

Anukai gasped. "Oh no!I'm-is that why you-!" She had never felt worse in her life. "I'm-sorry," she whispered hoarsely and folded herself around him as he cried until he couldn't cry anymore. Time stopped and every bad name she'd ever been called attacked her as she tried to console her old friend.

chapter thirty four

Her eyes popped open to the faint sound of singing.

The Eldercare women from the grandmother's church watched in shock as Danise stumbled out of a drug den towards the songs of praise they'd lifted up like warriors as they marched down blighted streets.

The lyrics Danise knew by heart lilted out of what was left of her once ethereal voice ecstatically as she marveled at the crystalline purity of the light outside before she crashed to the ground at their feet, the needle still precariously in her arm as she sang hollowly in the gutter. What had been choking her was dead due to the gunk she had injected into them both.

"Get up." her inner child ordered as screams of surprised praise erupted around her.

"Get up! You aren't done yet. Neither is the Lord-" the prayer warriors roared as she blacked out to the sound of ambulances arriving on site.

Danise screamed as the electricity slammed through her chest then passed back out. When she came to she found herself tied to a bed in a white padded room. She screamed at the top of her lungs.

The delirium and withdrawal sweats started as the drying out began.

chapter thirty five

"Look. I don't know a thing about this Jesus you all say you serve-" the doctor said abruptly, then paused.

"What I do know is this: Two minutes more walking around with that much gunk in her, her system would have irreparably shut down." he murmured. "What I do know is how hard it is to get ambulances to even go over there due to the headaches anyone from over there brings into the hospitals around here.. .and tonight one just happened to be turning the corner as one of you went to call 911 and you were able to flag it down. If this wasn't a case of God actually intervening, then I do not know what would be." The doctor said simply.

He turned and found Danise's mother in the crush of prayed up old folks. "She's weak. On every level, ma'am. And I am...so sorry for...For all the losses that seem to be befalling you one after another... but your daughter is going to make it. She's going to have to sweat it out. But she's going to be okay. I feel that in my heart. Maybe that's God....finally speaking to me." he whispered, staring off into the distance. "I see enough hell in here to forget he even exists sometimes. But your Danise.. .and all your...prayer warriors, your friends... reminded me he does tonight."

He started to walk off then stopped. "Your daughter is a fighter. Remind her of that every time she looks like she's starting to forget." The church men and women who had waited with her for hours to speak with the opioid specialist looked on solemnly as the doctor hugged Danise's stricken mother.

chapter thirty six

The woman woke up surrounded by padded white that pulsed out at her as she groggily shook her head and waited for her spirit to still.

Nestled into the crook of her arm was a passed-out little boy in tube socks and little boy long-johns that were unevenly shoved up against his ashy, crooked calves. The pristine white tank he had on was pushed up, his belly on the cheek of a wild-haired little girl in a eyelet princess nightgown sprawled across him, as dead to the space around her as he was.

Bleary-eyed, the woman's own body registered. She too was clothed in all white, an air-spun pair of white-washed doctor's scrubs and a filmy camisole the outlines of her nipples were visible through.

She inched from under the kids, intent on finding out what else there was in the space besides her and them. The air fought against her every move. She willed the cells in her body to split ranks and counter-attack whatever was holding her down. Instinctively she stretched out her fingers along the cushiony floor and found some give in the atmosphere, then slid her arm slowly across, pressing up against whatever was intent on keeping her down in hopes it'd not notice her discovery. She did her best to make contact with some semblance of anything- a wall, a seam, but found nothing.

The atmosphere slapped her face, aware of the subterfuge. A sharp cry erupted out of her chest. Her eyes slammed shut as angry, confused tears sprung up.

"They don't like that-" she heard whispered hoarsely into the space around her.

The sound of the soft voice stilled the chaos that roared in her head and the pressure in the air around her diminished. When she opened her eyes again the little boy and girl were standing before her, sleepily wiping their eyes and noses.

"They don't like what?" the woman unintentionally snapped as she stood up, looming over the two of them as she wiped at her own tears. She didn't realize that they were blood as she dragged the back of her soiled hand across her chest absently. The kids raised their eyebrows, momentarily bewildered by the blood, then regained their composure and spoke in unison.

"When you reach out-" the children said softly.
"...And who are They? No- You know what?- I don't even care anymore- I don't even know who you two are-I don't know any of this-" she coughed and waved them away angrily. They didn't budge. She sighed, trying to control herself as anger washed over her. "Where is Dr. Eudaimon?! Why are you here anyway?!" she snapped.

"They said you don't need-" the little boy started but the little girl shushed him. The children looked at each other. The woman roughly raked her hand up through another stream of bloody tears into her pristinely pressed hair, confused. "But we were in his- I was with-Everything was-"

She looked around at the white nervously. It seemed to glare at her balefully. The woman dropped her arms down helplessly. "Where are we?" she spat.

"The only place you see differently from-" the little boy whispered.
"-and really understand," the little girl cut in and lazily stuck

her left thumb in her mouth.

"And where-" Danise growled as her patience grew thin, "Where is that?"

"Nowhere-" the little girl sung.
The little boy chimed in "Now here-" at the same time.

"And why am I now here in nowhere-" the woman asked as she looked around at nothing.

"You Overdosed. Toooo much smack, Danise." they said just left of in unison. The little girl's voice lilted along slowly behind the rustle of air whistling from unseen holes in the boy's lungs.

"You gotta decide if you're going to live-" the little boy started,

"Or die...in here," the girl whispered softly as she reached out and pushed the thighs of the woman backwards until she sat down. Suddenly the two children loomed over her the way she had over them what felt like an eternity ago. "When it's your time- to go-you know," they said at the same time.

"It's not time-" Danise whispered nervously as she tried to stand back up against dizziness. Padded white spooled out forever in every direction she looked. "It's. Not. Time. I'm okay- I'm not going to do anything-bad- It's-not that- See! I made it this time-I only went back to-"

The woman looked down. Two jagged lines crawled up from her wrists to the inside of her elbows, faint like over- extended life-lines "Wait- no, no- that's not what I did- I- I only went back in to-to-I didn't do this-" Danise stammered, bewildered by the cuts on her arms.

"Oh Yes you did!" the little boy hissed. "Look what you

already did to me!" he exploded . His tank soaked through with blood as he kicked at the woman. The little girl in eyelet tried to hold him back. A gash opened on his forehead and he began to bleed out violently, struggling against the grip of his blood-drenched friend.

"You Dino-Doctor promised me you'd be Okay! But you're here! You promised never to come back here- You lied! I'll never trust you again! I'll never believe you again!"

"No, Gah- No! You don't understand! I didn't- I Mean I had to ...to-" she cried out as why she'd shot up evaporated from her memory. The bewildered woman cowered away from the two blood-soaked children as slashes up her arms unfurled. Blood gushed everywhere. Shell-shocked, she slowly crawled towards where the corner would've been if it had actually existed, towards the last of the white as the sudden bloodbath soaked into the padding and slowly spread across where there would have been walls, floor and ceiling in the space. The woman retched at the sight of the blood.

"I'm not going to do it- I'm not going to-" she repeated as the red in the room devoured more and more of the white. She closed her eyes against the wetness of it all, unable to bear it. When she reopened them everything including their skins and hair were drenched in an opaque, pure red, including the whites of their eyes.

The glare from the switch of the spectrum from white to red made her heady, but at least none of it was wet. She pressed her head into the padded floor as she continued to pull herself away from the still flailing little boy on her hands and knees, her head twisted awkwardly towards them.

"Please-" the little girl cried out as she struggled against the hell-bent little boy. "Please just -just come back-don't leave him like this- I can't handle-him like this- I'm too small-" The little girl swung herself around and slammed her chest into his and knocked him back, wrapping her spindly arms around him as they went flying.

"She's going to come back- she's going to, I promise! She will!" the little girl whispered repetitively as he screamed, trying to lash out at Danise around his friend. "She's going to come back-and help you-" the little girl whispered, "aren't you?"

Danise slumped into a pile of bent arms and legs and nodded her head. "I promise I won't do this again- no matter how bad it gets - No matter what-"

"See-" the little girl sighed. "I told you-you're gonna be Okay," she whispered to the boy who slowly stopped fighting against her and eyed the hunched over woman warily. "She's not going to do anything bad this time- she is gonna go back, and take care you, take care of everything- she will not- won't trap us in here this time- she's going to do different this time- She-She's going to get out of here different- as different as it takes to never come back again..." the girl whispered.

She inched back over towards the woman with the little boy cagily behind her. They stood uneasily next to the woman as the little girl reached out and patted the grown-up lady gently on her crown like she was a scared puppy.

"She's going to be alright- this time- she'll go back and- and she won't-fail- we're all going to make it-through-"

The little boy got on his knees as he hesitantly raised his hand and placed it gently on the side of the woman's cheek.

"Make it all the way home- No matter what it takes," he hissed nervously at the woman as she rocked herself back and forth.

The little girl knelt down next to him and pressed her forehead into the woman's back, swaying softly with them until they all fell asleep, curled up as the red faded back out to white before dissolving, with all of them in it.

chapter thirty seven

Gabryl reached out and gratefully stroked Anukai's hair under the cherry tree. It began to spiral out even more wildly. Anukai bit down on her lip and looked away from the reflection of her housed in his eyes shamefully.

"Now I'm going to get in trouble cause my hair is messed up! Look what you did!" she cried out softly as her hand flew up to her head. His eyes got so sad that he looked as if he could have done anything to make her feel better, he would have done it. His brain raced as he saw her body shake with tears that wouldn't materialize out into the world that was supposed to be more real.

"I'll do your hair- I did it before remember?" he said. Anukai looked at him wide-eyed as memories that didn't make sense nipped at the side of her face. She swatted them away without saying a word, then jumped up.

"I have to go to school." she whispered as this strange sense of calm settled down over her. she felt horrible because suddenly she knew exactly what she had to do. "Look-" she started, "I can't go all the way back- I -It's not mines anymore-I gave it up- I don't belong to it anymore- and I- I'm so sorry about your Grandpere and-" her heart shook, "and oh my-you had a- a little brother, too? But I- I can't- too much goes wrong when I don't pay attention here- Please leave me alone, Gabryl."

The bell for school rang and she ran off, wiping away her tears. She sat down at her desk, laid her head down and quietly cried herself to sleep at the back of the room within five minutes.

chapter thirty eight

Gabryl tried to understand as he sat in the dirt and let his tears fall. He slammed his eyes shut in an attempt to go back home.

When he opened them he was still in Anukai's real world.

A tear slid down his nose onto the ground next to what she'd been drawing in the dirt when he'd appeared beside her.

He wiped at his nose as he inspected it, his right hand absently tracing a copy of it next to the one she'd drawn, line by line, box, by box. He laid down next to it and peered at the earth. Each porous clump of green grass stood out in relief against the fractured blue sky that spilled over the horizon line behind it as he fell asleep.

"How did it go with your little jungle friend?" Gabryl's grandmother rattled as he came out of his stupor.

He shrugged. "How's-" he asked tentatively.

"She's waiting for you. You want me to-"
"I'll be okay grandma."
"I know, baby- You're my Strong boy. And your mama feels- much better. She's really going to be okay-it just might take some time before she's ..." his grandmother whispered softly.

"I know." he whispered woodenly.

chapter thirty nine

Anukai barreled out of another boring day of being ostracized at school. She paused and warily looked back over towards the tree she'd gotten recess detention for sitting too long under.

She looked down the block in the direction of her house, then back at the only cherry tree she technically had left. She raced back up the hill and plopped down again, crossing her fingers that something would happen, that maybe, even after she had told him to go he hadn't listened to her and was somehow still there so she wouldn't have to go home just yet.

She got on her hands and knees in the grass and squeezed her eyes shut, not realizing that she was praying to God for a friend, praying that God hadn't let her send him away, that he was real, and just far away like he'd said. She opened her eyes. Disappointment wheezed out of her like a broken squeeze-toy stepped on one too many times.

As she sprawled sadly in the grass, a weird little white girl came up to the tree with glasses and thick brown French braids plaited into her hair so tightly that her scalp glowed pink.

Anukai looked up and grunted as the girl wrapped her arms around the tree and looked down at the lanky black girl with the wild hair she'd seen get into fight after fight for most of the school year. She smiled, partially because she always drew blood when she fought the bullies, and grunted back as Anukai looked past her at the red posies in bloom beyond the trees.

The little girl started blowing spit bubbles for no reason whatsoever, bubbles that Anukai ignored until she repeatedly heard them pop. She looked up warily.

"What?" Anukai snapped defensively, not realizing how tired

she was until she opened her mouth. The little white girl blew another spit bubble and spoke as it popped.

"Nothing...you're just where I sit after school when I don't want to go home-" the girl said plainly, "It's okay though- I don't mind you being in it, it's a good spot."

Anukai's curiosity got the best of her."Why don't you want to go home?" she asked, self-consciously blowing a spit bubble of her own.

"Pop." The girl said at the same time her newest bubble popped.

Anukai looked at her, confused. The girl wiped absently at her pressed white Peter Pan collar and dug the toe of her generic converses into the dirt before saying it again. "Pop. My dad. He drinks while I'm at school...so he won't remember what he...does...after-" the little girl looked away.

"Did you ever tell anybody?" Anukai asked sullenly, instantly understanding.

"...I just told you," the little girl trilled happily as she blew another bubble and popped it with her tongue. "Because I can tell you don't want to go home either. But yeah, I told. My grandmother got really red and then hit me until I agreed that I imagined it- so I just don't think about it anymore."

"Now I just stay away til mom comes home--it's the only thing that seems to work-" she paused and looked at the ground. " Hey! What's that? Did you do those?" she asked, pointing with her extended toe towards the dirt.

Anukai cocked her head to the side and saw the happiness symbol she'd drawn with her finger earlier that morning. One just like it was pushed into the dirt beside it.

Anukai's mouth dropped open. She shut it as she looked up at the girl and gauged her before saying anything.

"It means happiness," Anukai whispered, trying to sound casual, acting as if she only saw one of them just in case. "I did it this morning."

The little white girl tugged on one of her french braids as she knelt down to get a closer look, the biggest spit bubble yet balanced on the rim of her mouth. "Both of them? Or does that mean it's twice as happy since there's two of them?" she asked, an innocent smile in her eyes.

Anukai's face softened as she nodded, weirded out that the little girl saw both of them. "I guess so- I guess it does." she whispered, elated.

Anukai suddenly spit in her hands and pressed both of them into the dirt, a palm over each symbol, blowing her own spit bubble as she grinned up at the sky then dragged each hand down its opposite arm, blushing as she openly hugged herself. The little white girl shrugged her shoulders as the school bell rang again, letting her know that her mother should be home to deal with her drunken dad by now.

"Whatever floats your boat," she laughed as she stood up to walk away. "See you tomorrow?" she asked shyly. Anukai shook her head yes as a happy scowl of surprise rose up.

 Someone was actually planning on seeing her the next day? And in front of people too?! And she was real *and* saw the second symbol that Gabryl must've drawn after Anukai had gone into school?!

It happily blew her mind.

They blew spit bubbles at each other again and parted ways, both heading into their respective hells a little stronger than they'd been before.

chapter forty

Gabryl entered the room his mom was propped up in but stayed around the doorjamb.

"Hi momma," he whispered. She looked up and smiled at him like little baby Jesus.

" Hi Baby!" she cooed before she started to ramble about what a beautiful day the Lord had made for them all to enjoy.

She'd come back a completely different person due to Jesus and whatever they'd given her to keep her clean.

And whoever this new person was, Gabryl couldn't bear to be in the room with for more than fifteen minutes without wanting to scream. He nodded along as she talked about scriptures, then excused himself. "Momma, I am glad you feel better...I gotta go do homework."

"Okay Gah-" she started to call him by his nickname then abruptly stopped. Gabryl perked up until he saw the shadow flit across his mother's face. She coughed a little. "Okay- okay.. .baby~" she stammered, confused by the word stuck in her throat.

Crestfallen and inexplicably angry, Gabryl excused himself from the presence of whomever had replaced his mother in her body and went back to his room.

chapter forty one

Anukai refused to cry.

The tender-headed child's scalp was raw from the rough washing the mother had just put her through, throat rammed into the stainless steel rim of the kitchen sink so often that there was a slight bruise. The blustering heat of the blow- dryer with the chipped comb attachment tore through 18 inches of naturally curly hair until it had begun to look like carded black wool. The scabs from last month's washing gave way under the force and new puss rose up and spread like warm glue while the hair cooled.

"You and this damn...hair-" the thin-haired Mother griped. She tried to keep the little girl's hair out of the way with one hand as she vainly parted it with her weaker hand.

"What did you do to it?! I come home from that fucking job only to have to be bothered with this fucking chore-" the mother seethed as she angrily balanced her elbow on the little girl's head, her forearm pressed to the hair that seemed to fight against her. Anukai hunched down deeper as she tried not to wince against the pain as the mother harshly ripped the comb across her scalp again and again. The mother's arm slipped so that the hair got away from her and defiantly fused back together as if it had never been parted.

"Sonafabitch!" the mother cursed as she slammed the comb full-force into the little girl's head, fully intending to hurt her. The force of the hit bounced back off of the girl's hair as if a force-field had sprung up around her. The mother roughly scratched herself on the collarbone. The little girl tried to swallow her snicker a second too late.

"Oh! It's funny to you, huh?! You and this fucking hair!" the mother howled as she slammed the teeth of the comb into and across the little girl's forehead, breaking the skin.

The little girl yowled as she cowered away from the sparks that shot out of the mother's eyes. Empowered by the child's screams, the mother threw the comb at the little girl and hissed. "You know what?! I'm done! You're big enough! Do your own fucking hair!"

Relief spread across her face, but the little girl was quick to hide it before the mother could see it and steal her joy. She narrowed her eyes through tears, grabbed the comb and ran upstairs towards the only bathroom door in the house that could be locked.

"Go ahead you little beast! You'll look even more like a fucking banshee on your own- You'll see! I'm through!" the mother called out. "At least your crazy daddy can't say shit to me about it! Should have stuck around to do that shit!! Who in this family even has hair like that? Me and Flower? We've got good hair!" the mother screamed after Anukai as she dabbed absently at the droplets of her own blood drawn by her own attack.

chapter forty two

"Iont' care if I look like a banshee…As long as she never touches my hair again-" the little girl pouted as she ran into the bathroom.

She gently locked the door behind her and turned on the water softly, watching it as it tumbled out of the tap into the pristine white, claw-footed bathtub. Anukai danced her fingers in the water and zoned out. She pressed her face against the clammy outside of the tub and let it cool her cheek before she sleepily caught sight of the falling water again.

Outside, the new kids on the block her age happily howled up and down the street. Eventually it faded into the background, replaced instead with metallic-sounding birds chirping. The little girl began clucking to herself in an thoughtless ape of the blue-jays and robins arguing over branches in the last standing trees out back.

Hypnotized into better layers of thoughts and life, her eyes began to white out as she almost forgot why she was hiding in the bathroom to begin with. By the time the tub was quietly filled, the sun had shifted and began to drop heavy golden rays of light across the surface of the water and the mirror on the dressing table alongside the tub.

Anukai slowly stood up and slipped down into the depths of the water fully dressed, her hands doing their best to hold on as the water displaced by the weight of her spilled over out onto the floor. As she situated herself, waves as large as tsunamis from an internal point of view crashed into her stomach, then chest, and finally throat.

The gnarled mass of hair relaxed in the humidity of the bathroom and peace fully hit the child. Her hair danced gingerly across the water as if it were trying to decide whether or not to submerge a strand at a time.

The gentle lap of the oceanic waves against her voice-box made her laugh softly as her hair reverted to ringlets. The sound echoed in the tiled space around her.

She slowly let her fingers slip under the surface of the water and sink as much as they could before they floated gently back up. Her legs stretched out in front of her as the rubber- capped tips of her still sneaker- encased feet floated up at the far end of the tub. She let the lightness of her legs pull her hips forward and tilted her head back until all of her was completely under the waves except her nose, mouth and wide-opened eyes. She tentatively let her mouth go slack and let some of the water flow in.

A muffled sound called out across the room. The water garbled it but she knew she'd heard something. She turned her head and lifted an ear above the water. A voice called out again tremulously from the far corner of the room.

"Don't go-Don't leave me-not like this-" Gabryl said hoarsely. He crawled out of the mirror, tip-toed over to the tub and peered in. The little girl's hair rippled underwater like a giant halo of shimmering seaweed. "Don't let them win by giving up." he continued softly and knelt beside the tub.

"I'm not leaving," she snapped underwater, "I'm washing the puss out of my hair. She's never doing my hair again."

Anukai scowled defiantly and submerged her exposed ear back under the water, closing her eyes so as not to hear or see anything to the contrary of what she'd decided. "She said it herself, and she's sticking to it-even if it kills me-"

The little boy brushed off the tone in her voice and smiled as he lowered his face into the tub.

"Let me wash it again," he whispered underwater. It boomed in her ears and she shot straight up out of the water. Rivulets coursed down her face as she scowled at him.

"No! Nobody's touching my hair ever again!!"

She narrowed her eyes. "And I told you! I'm not playing with you anymore" she spat, forgetting how happy she'd been over double happiness what felt like a lifetime ago. He brushed her bad mood that landed on him off and spoke to her calmly.

"I told you, I'm not leaving." he smiled at her. She glowered back at him. "I won't touch your hair...won't touch you if you don't want me to-but I'm not going away. You don't even have to talk to me if you don't want to, but I'm not going away."

"Just leave me alone!" the little girl whined. "No...because... I love you," he whispered, "And I promised before I was not going to leave you."

"It doesn't matter anymore, Gabryl!" she cried out softly. "You can't help me -"

"I don't care-I can still Be here-for you-" Gabryl cut her off crossly. "I'm not leaving," he whispered as he slid into the other end of the tub in all his clothes as well, "...because I promised! And I keep my promises! I don't care if you changed your mind- Change it back!"

He quickly dunked himself under the waves with his eyes wide open so as not to lose sight of his old friend. More water spilled onto the bathroom floor. They sat at opposing ends of the tub, glaring at each other.

"No! I need you to go away, Gabryl."the little girl cried. "It's time for me to grow up- I can't play with you anymore! I need to grow up so I can get out of here-"

"You can grow up without sending me away! Why do I have to go? Nobody else can see me anyway-" he yelled. "I'm not going anywhere! I'm not leaving you!" he glowered at her as if it were taking every bit of his will not to lunge at her and hang on for dear life.

The light in the room changed. Suddenly the little girl's face looked very old. "Then I have to leave you." she whispered plainly.

Before he could stop her, she plunged her head backwards into the tub and quickly inhaled as much water as she could before blacking out as he furiously tried to pull her back up out of it.

chapter forty three

She opened her eyes underwater and caught sight of her knees above the surface of it.

The bathroom was full of steam over as she rose up out of the tub. She wrapped a big towel around her wet hair then absently wiped at the mirror. The steam threatened to re-fog it as quickly as she wiped it away. She peered into her reflection with amazement as she popped open a bottle of niacin, swallowed another handful of tablets, then swigged from the water bottle she'd taken into the tub with her.

Her unkempt eyebrows wildly shot off the sides of her face as if she were in the perpetual state of issuing a dare. The nose that was the only proof she'd ever had of being related by blood to the dysfunctional brood she'd been raised in had been grown into so much so that it was almost unrecognizable as her father's.

Her eyes sparkled, reflecting the tiny droplets of moisture strewn across her lashes back at her as the niacin flush rose up across her skin. Her head rolled back as her body was rocked with the internal explosions of heat. She didn't fight the blush-grin.

When teenaged Anukai opened her eyes, two Chinese characters for happiness were scrawled across the mirror.

She wiped at the mirror again before she reached over the tub and threw open the window. Cold air pushed its way into the room as the snow on the window-sill started to melt. She absently reached her hand into the tub and unplugged it before settling back down at the dressing table.

She looked down at her fully-formed body and smiled sheepishly at her own reflection. Anukai cut her eyes at the body of the little boy dead man's floating in the tub as the bathwater drained away.

"Stop it." she murmured softly, "I'm too old for this. I'm not paying any attention to you."

"You don't have to," a gravelly voice murmured. An almost grown-up Gabryl sat up, climbed out of the tub and pulsed into view directly behind her right shoulder in the mirror.

He attempted not to look down at the de facto nudist his no longer little friend had matured into because it distracted him from the focus necessary to patch into her world. The air shook with electricity as he slid closer and closer to her until the damp skin of his inner thighs was all but pressed up alongside hers.

"We're almost old, aren't we?" he whispered.

Anukai nodded and flicked open her eyes, a vulnerable look etched into the features of the pretty much grown-up face she looked out of. The irises began to pulse and fade as she tried to lock onto the space where his eyebrows attempted to appear. "So that means you're about to come and find me, right?" he whispered.

She closed her eyes again as his almost adult face flashed fully into view in the mirror for a split second. "How am I going to come find you when you don't really exist-" she sighed.

"You promised me," Gabryl murmured, "Just like I promised you I wouldn't leave you- And I didn't, did I?"

"You don't exist, Gabryl," she snapped softly.

"How you going to tell me I don't exist-" he started as she whirled around, cutting him off.

"Then where are you? Huh! Where are you? You're talking to me but I don't see a damn-" she got caught off guard by the sight of herself flailing angrily around in the mirror, sucked air through her teeth and continued.

"You don't exist and I'm not coming anywhere to find you. I'm going to school," she stated plainly as she shook out her hair, trying to ignore the very real sensation of his breath on her neck. "And stop doing that!" she snapped as she waved his face away from her neck. Gabryl snorted, which took a layer off of her bravado. "I'm going to school-" she whispered, voice faltering.

"You wouldn't have to cut classes just to get a moment's peace after this war zone if you came to find me," he mumbled hoarsely as he knit his brows dramatically.

"You don't even have a home, last you were telling me," Anukai snorted. "Ain't you on a couch cuzza Jesus?"

"If you don't believe I'm for real, why you holding onto the shit I say to you, Anukai?" Gabryl chuckled, a triumphant look in his eyes as he solidified in front of her.

"Because you don't let me sleep!" she yelped.

Gabryl waved her complaints off. "You know exactly what-what to do to shut me up..." he insinuated. Anukai reared up as if she were about to blast him. He blushed "I meant find me! Come and find me! And See! Look at where your mind went-And if you get pregnant here I swear to whatever I'm going to find you and kill the both of-"

Anukai rolled her eyes and walked out the bathroom back to her room " I'm going to school. Leave. Me. Alone."

"Leave-me-alone" Gabryl mimicked. "Nah! Not till you get off your ass and come find me!"

Anukai spun around as she struggled into her underwear and combat boots. "Are you implying I should not finish school, run away from home, and live on the streets of all the big cities of America in search of your supposedly real ass?" she asked sweetly. "Why not tell me exactly where you are?"

He looked up from her feet, confused by her stepping into her underwear after her boots the way he was every time she got dressed in front of him.

"What?" he asked cagily, unable as usual to remember who, what, or where he was whenever the time came for him to actually tell her so she'd know where to look.

Anukai rolled her eyes, pulled on the overalls she'd cut into a mini-dress of sorts, threw on a bright green dickey knit by her grandmother atop it and shrugged into one of her father's leather car coats he had left behind.

She glared at Gabryl, bounded down the stairs and out the door towards school, hopefully in time for art class or physics, depending on the days she no longer bothered trying to keep straight.

"New York!" he howled from the pit of his stomach as he watched her turn the block from her window. "I'm in fucking New York!" he screamed in her room angrily.

Whatever had blocked his mouth eased up so he could breathe as curse words flooded the surface of his skin.

The end.

ABOUT THE AUTHOR

Author and multimedia artist Angel Brynner has marched to the beat of her own drum across the arts for over two decades. After formal training with the vanguard of the menswear industry she helmed her own line of men's clothing and produced events for the collection in the club scenes of New York and Tokyo.

She became quietly known for the futuristic cautionary tales back-dropping her collections, taking over clubs and the guerilla-marketing style she used to slam her vision into the hearts of her fans. While being sponsored by Multinational companies desiring audience with her underground tribe, she returned from Japan to her hometown to press charges against a pedophile before the statute of limitations ran out.

Cast as a vigilante by a corrupt sex crimes unit for trying to protect another child from the same attacker, during the media onslaught against the first brave adults to come forward and press charges against the Catholic priests that had abused them as children she was hit with a vision of all those already lost in a sick war on kids no one talked about.

She committed herself & her art to doing something about it.

The grievechronic universe was forged in the fires of imagining the Armageddon that would erupt through a generation of kids who had finally had enough abuse at the hands of adults and banded together under their grievances.
The epic spiritual, metaphysical, and historical implications of such an event played out on every level- from the hellish norms that caused it to what would be called heaven by such a broken world- made her head spin.

Published by Kokopellima Press, each free-standing installment of grievechronic Is a take-no- prisoners tale.

Alongside AOLAB[the active-art series featuring the multimedia work that fed Eutaxis, Ecclesia, Exodus, Erebus, Exist and the kinetic collection of novels that follow them], Angel Brynner's books are the culmination of an artistic journey many years in the making, all leading to a mysterious future project entitled **Transcendence.**

Eutaxis. /Grievechronic\...
Angel Brynner
2h 44m

ECCLESIA. /grievechronic...
Angel BRYNNER
3h 3m

EXODUS. /grievechronic\...
Angel BRYNNER
2h 21m

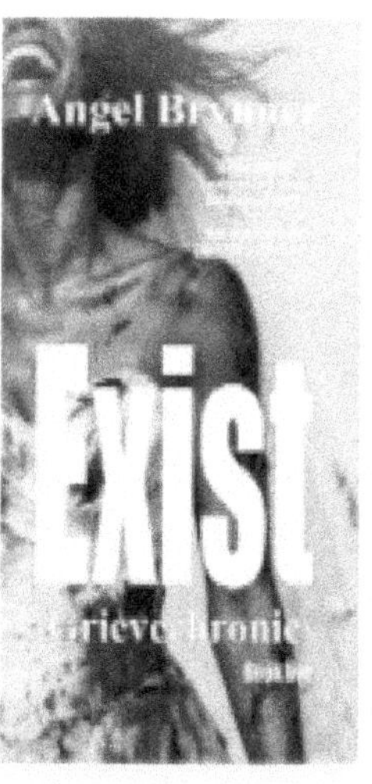

EREBUS./grievechronic\...
Angel Brynner
2h 56m

EXIST. /grievechronic\ boo...
Angel Brynner
2h 36m

ESTHESIS. /grievechronic...
Angel Brynner
2h 47m

THE NINTH (& LATEST) ENTRY TO THE / GRIEVECHRONIC\ UNIVERSE

False utopias look like heaven when they exist inside of you, but the spell breaks when you fall. Halcyon days harbor great space for healing if they can stand being held up to the light. The memories we run and hide in may overlap or coincide, but underneath each pleasing space is all that we have yet to face. Hiding bodies to embrace the good is par for the course. But those bones must live again in order to truly break free. The good goes down in spite of what you have to ignore to be grateful for it, but ignoring shit doesn't make anything really go away….and going away only goes so far.

"It looks like Heaven." That may be true. But don't forget what you've gone through

Elysum
before or after the fall may never have been Paradise at all.

ISBN 978-1-950077-83-0
52000
9 781950 077830

Angel Brynner
ELYSIUM
/grievechronic\
Now available in paperback
Everywhere.